Wuthering Hearts

Other titles by Kay Woodward:

Jane Airhead

Wuthering Hearts

Kay Woodward

ANDERSEN PRESS • LONDON

First published in 2011 by
Andersen Press Limited
20 Vauxhall Bridge Road
London SW1V 2SA
www.andersenpress.co.uk

2 4 6 8 10 9 7 5 3 1

British Library Cataloguing in Publication Data available.

ISBN 978 1 84939 299 0

Typeset by Ellipsis Digital Limited, Glasgow
Printed and bound in Great Britain
by CPI Bookmarque, Croydon CR0 4TD

For Woody and Anya –
you're smashing

Chapter One

'Noooo!' wailed Emily, dramatically. It was Drama, after all. And if she couldn't get away with being dramatic in Drama, where could she get away with it? Besides, this was an emergency. Drama was required.

Uh-oh. Emily froze as Miss Edwards turned towards her, looking thunderous.

Ah. Apparently she couldn't get away with being dramatic here either.

In agonising slow motion the Drama teacher angled her Roman nose slowly downwards until she had a clear view over the top of gold, half-rimmed glasses. She switched on her death-ray stare.

Bzzzzzzt.

Emily's stomach lurched, but she kept her nerve. Some things were too important to ignore, and the idea of *Wuthering Heights* as the school play was one of them. Although, right now, the stunned faces of her classmates were telling Emily that her leading-lady strop might be a tiny bit OTT. She decided to tone it down a bit.

'Come on . . .' Emily said reasonably. '*Wuthering Heights* is so dark and depressing. It's always raining. And what about the characters? Everyone's called Cathy or Catherine or Cath or Kitty or Kat or Cate or, um . . . what's his name . . . ? Cliff? No, *Heath*cliff. He's a right charmer, isn't he? *Not*.'

There was an ominous silence as Emily wondered helplessly what a girl had to do around here to convince someone that *Wuthering Heights*, well, sucked. And she *had* to convince Miss Edwards of her mistake before it was too late. Frantically she scrabbled around for more ammo. 'And everyone marries their cousin and they're always miserable and soaking wet, like, all the time. Or dead. And—'

'Thank you for your eloquent critique, Miss Sparrow.' The teacher's tone was chilly. 'But if you're quite finished, I have a play to direct.'

Deep down Emily knew that her brief campaign was dead in the water, but she went for it anyway. 'Not quite finished, actually,' she said. 'What about the health and safety issues?' The road map of veins standing out on Miss Edwards' forehead made Emily's voice shoot up an octave. 'There is a lot of broken glass in *Wuthering Heights* . . .' she squeaked.

'Thank you, Emily,' said the Drama teacher with finality.

'No problem,' Emily whispered.

'For the love of Edward Cullen, will you shut up?' hissed Maia, from behind a cupped hand. 'I thought you wanted to *star* in the school play. If you don't quit whingeing, you won't even get a walk-on part.'

'I was only saying that I don't want to do *Wuthering Heights*,' Emily whispered back. 'It's not fair.'

Maia flung her eyes towards the polystyrene ceiling tiles before replying in an undertone. 'We're in Yorkshire,' she said. '*Wuthering Heights* is totally logical.'

'So's algebra,' grumbled Emily. 'I don't get that either.'

Two desks away Lexie Allinton carefully tucked

her ash-blonde hair behind one ear. 'Miss Edwards?' she said in an angelic voice. '*Wuthering Heights* is actually my favourite book, like, ever. I'd love to play Cathy. You know, the lead role? I just really relate to her. Miss, it feels like the perfect role for me.'

Emily felt as though a torrent of icy water had whooshed all over her. Playing the lead role in the school play was *her* dream. She was the one who longed to be an actress and who put in the hours, going to every workshop on offer, and actually *reading* plays. If Miss Edwards was dead set on forcing them to whinge and wail their way through *Wuthering Heights*, then the lead belonged to *her*.

Emily should be Cathy. Not Lexie.

But the other girl was already speaking earnestly about how she and Cathy were so alike that it was as if they were separated at birth. Emily realised too late that *Wuthering Heights* might be bad, but the thought of missing out on the lead was far, far worse.

'We're soul mates, miss,' Lexie went on. 'It's like the role was written for me.' She laid her hand on her heart as she spoke, looking totally sincere.

Personally Emily thought that if they were talking perfect roles here, then Lexie was more like the whining, posh Isabella than Cathy. Silently this time, she roared another *Noooo* as the chance of a lifetime slipped further and further away. Lexie had made her case beautifully. Emily had to give it to her – the girl was good.

Lexie Allinton wasn't just good. She was cool too. *She* was the girl that all of the other girls wanted to be. If Lexie liked someone, they were instantly promoted to the big league, which meant sleepovers and shopping trips and nail bars and evenings spent in her outdoor hot tub. But if Lexie didn't like someone, then it meant none of the above. And after an incident last term when Lexie's boyfriend happened to mention that he thought Emily was 'nice', the boyfriend had become an ex-boyfriend and Emily was permanently denied access to the popular big league. Not that she'd ever wanted to join anyway. Much.

Emily's desperation increased. She had to shut her rival up. 'But—'

Lexie, who was in the middle of telling everyone how feisty she and Cathy were, turned to glower at her. 'You've had your turn to speak,' she said. 'Why not let someone else have a go? We're talking about *Wuthering Heights*, not you.'

'Yeah?' muttered Sam Harrison. 'I thought *you*

were talking about *you*, Lexie?' He snorted at his own quick wit, elbowing a dark-haired boy Emily had never seen before. The boy was sitting slumped in the next chair, looking as if he'd rather be anywhere else but a steamed-up classroom in West Yorkshire on a wet autumn afternoon.

Wow. Emily stared at him, momentarily distracted from the twin disasters at hand. He might be frowning and looking totally dejected, but there was no escaping the fact that the boy was . . . well, gorgeous. 'Who is he?' she whispered to Maia. 'Where did he come from?'

'New boy,' replied Maia under her breath. 'Robert McBride. Looks a bit miserable. Sneaked in while you were having your hissy fit.'

Robert lifted heavy lids and scowled angrily in their direction, even though there was no way he could have heard them.

A dry gulp wedged in Emily's throat and she swallowed painfully. With regret she realised that the new boy didn't look the type to leap over desks and snog her any time soon. Even worse he wasn't the only one giving her the evils. Everyone seemed to be staring at her slack-jawed. And not in a wow-how-brave way either.

This wasn't going at all well.

'Ahem.' It was Miss Edwards, still looking mad. 'Are there any other votes against one of the world's greatest classics?' Her angry gaze mine-swept the classroom for objectors and she bared her teeth in a furious smile that dared them to speak, while simultaneously promising retribution for anyone who actually did.

No one spoke.

Clearly no one was as dumb as Emily Sparrow.

'Excellent,' said Miss Edwards. 'Then, by an overwhelming majority, I'd like to announce that this year's Christmas play will be based on the novel *Wuthering Heights* written by the brilliant Emily Brontë, our local nineteenth-century celeb. It will be adapted for the stage by my good self. Auditions start next Monday at four o'clock sharp, and Year Ten Drama pupils are strongly advised to come along.' She flared her nostrils at them. 'For the hard of understanding, that means that you will all be involved in the production. All of you.' She turned to Emily, smiling with a vinegary sweetness. 'That includes you, Miss Sparrow. Don't be late.'

Emily gave a leaden nod. Her mini uprising against *Wuthering Heights* was over and already she had a new battle: how to make sure that *she* – and not Lexie – was Cathy. The big question was, how she could stop the girl who always got her own way from, well . . . getting her own way again?

'Emily . . . ?'

She had almost forgotten that the teacher was there. 'Hmm?'

'You have read the book, haven't you? *Wuthering Heights*, I mean. It's just that you sound so knowledgeable about it that I thought you must've.'

'Yes!' This was outrageous. Of course Emily had read it. How dare Miss Edwards suggest otherwise? *Whoosh*. A hot wave of guilt flooded over her. *Oh. Oh dear.* Yes, she had started it – the summer before last while trapped inside a leaky tent in Brittany – but she hadn't actually finished it. So if they were being purist about this . . . No, she hadn't read *all* of it.

'I've read the first three or four . . . um . . . pages,' Emily admitted, seriously starting to wish that she'd never said anything about the stupid book. She tried to recover the situation. 'But that was enough. I got tonnes of stuff from those first few pages: imagery, metaphors . . . you know, masses of literary . . . um . . . literary-ness. So I've nearly read it. And I did watch the whole thing on TV last year. The two-part special, I mean. Both parts. So it's like I've read the whole thing.' She bit her lip. 'Sort of.'

Oh no. Everyone was watching, including the new boy who looked as if he were witnessing a road traffic accident – shocked, but unable to tear his eyes away from the horror of her public humiliation. Lexie was staring at her with ill-disguised glee.

'May I suggest you *sort of* read it all the way through?' said Miss Edwards. She couldn't have looked any more triumphant if she'd just won an Oscar. 'Then you can tell me that it *sucks*.'

Chapter Two

Emily headed through the rain towards home, grumbling to herself. She usually walked some of the way with Maia, but the end-of-school bell had hardly pinged before her best friend was sprinting towards town with a cheery wave and a promise to TXT U L8R. Maia could spot a strop coming and she wasn't hanging around. Emily didn't blame her. She half wished that she could walk home without her angry self too.

Emily stomped past DVDeez and the half-day-closed Coopers' Newsagent, but by the time she reached the old disused mill, its many windows starred with holes, she was starting to run and she sprinted up the last two streets, feeling the stress of her day falling away. Home at last, she pushed open the gate with a spirited *bang* and headed for the back door. Light glowed through the dimpled window. Good. Someone was in.

Blown inside with a flurry of autumn leaves, Emily saw Dad. Result. He'd want to know all about her day. His silver-grey head was bent over the kitchen table as he stared accusingly at the whirring laptop, which was marooned in a sea of paperwork. As Emily slammed the back door, he peered up at her, his tanned face crinkling into a smile.

'Be a love,' he said. 'Put the kettle on?'

'I can't,' Emily smirked. 'It won't fit.'

Dad did his trademark double-bass chortle. 'Good day?' he asked.

Emily flipped the kettle switch, dumped her school bag and wriggled out of her soggy coat before replying. 'Well—'

'Deep thing with water in it.' He was as quick as a flash.

Emily groaned. If he was in full-on Dad-joke mode, he could go on for hours and there'd be no chance of off-loading about the play. Not that she really minded. She could do with a laugh.

Dad was great. He danced like a relic from the 1980s, but he didn't interfere much. He was too busy doing other stuff, for a start. His proper job was working with young offenders, but in his spare time he led the local scout group. Father to two daughters, she often wondered if the thirty-odd boys were a relief from the girliness at home – but if they were, Dad politely avoided mentioning it. And when he wasn't doing any of the above, he somehow found the time to squeeze in random good deeds, like sorting out the neighbour's wi-fi or fixing a leaky gutter. This was all great, but it did mean that Dad wasn't around much – something Mum had cited as one of their countless 'irreconcilable differences'. Emily's parents might have had the sort of wild, passionate romance that they made films about – something they both admitted – but their divorce had been beyond awful. Emily shuddered as she remembered it and quickly handed over Dad's tea.

'Ahhhhh,' he sighed, post-slurp. 'So was today ace, wicked or sick?' He began scrawling ticks and scribbling in boxes on a very long form.

'*Dad* . . .' Emily sighed. 'Act your age, please. And besides, it wasn't any of those things. It was rubbish.'

'Excellent,' said Dad vaguely. He carried on ticking. 'Keep up the good work. Jenna's going to be late back from school. Something to do with the school play, I think.'

Emily's younger sister – by two years, nine months, ten days and seventeen hours, give or take a millisecond – was into hair straighteners, ballet and hip hop. 'Dad, that was *me*,' she said. 'Maybe ballet?' But the lack of response told Emily that she'd already lost him, and it was no good talking to Dad when he was working; he couldn't multitask to save his life. So, giving his earlobe a farewell flick as she passed, she left him to it and wandered out of the kitchen into the hall.

Emily loved her home, even though it wasn't big and glamorous like Lexie's. Originally it had been a tiny miner's cottage, but it now looked more like an advert for how *not* to renovate a house. It had weirdly shaped rooms and a patchwork roof. The walls were so wonky that pictures refused to hang straight, tilting mysteriously within seconds of being nudged back into place. In the dimly lit and wood-panelled hall, the noisy oak floor was uneven, with a surprise micro step halfway along to catch out unsuspecting visitors, and Dad.

The staircase on the right led upwards to the

bedrooms. But Emily knew that if she went that way, she would have to start inventing reasons not to do her homework, and besides, she still needed to tell someone about the whole *Wuthering Heights* debacle. Resolutely she headed past the cosy living room and the dining room that they never used – partly because it was where Mum had once thrown Dad's dinner at the wall, but mostly because there was no radiator and it was freezing – to the door at the far end of the hall and the narrow flight of stairs behind it. Slowly Emily began to climb.

'Yoohoo!' she called.

'I'm up here, dear!' warbled a bird-like voice. 'Just watching that game show where everyone falls in the water . . . Oh, there goes another one!' There was the sound of gentle whooping from upstairs.

Emily jogged up the final few steps and knocked on the old wooden door at the top, before letting herself in.

'Hello, dear!' The old lady who sat there gripping the remote was tiny, with watery blue-green eyes and cheeks that were slightly furry, like the skin of a ripe peach. Her ebony hair was smoothed into a French pleat that prickled with Kirby grips and even though she had to be seventy or more –

they were fed up of asking how old she was – she didn't have a single grey hair. Not one.

Emily flopped onto the chintz sofa and snuggled into its marshmallowy depths, instantly feeling at home.

This had once been a large, airy studio where Mum painted – when she wasn't rowing with Dad, or making up with him. After Mum left there was a brief, horrible hiatus, when all Dad seemed to do was drink tea and stare at the television. Then Great-aunt Olive arrived. She became Auntie Olive almost at once, and then Auntie O.

'Why don't I just stay on, dear?' Auntie O had said to Dad after she'd been there a fortnight. 'You'll be needing a babysitter now *she's* hiked off.'

Emily and Jenna had held their breath, hoping Dad would make the right decision.

He did. She stayed. And Dad transformed the studio into a chintz wonderland with its own tiny living room, tinier bedroom, kitchen and microscopic bathroom, aka the Granny Annexe.

The girls missed their mum, really missed her. But they didn't miss the arguments and the slamming doors. And Mum was so amazingly happy now that she was fulfilling her lifelong ambition of being an air stewardess. She had hooked up with a good-looking pilot pretty much straight away and now she lived with him in a blissfully argument-free two-bedroom flat in Fulham, flying long haul out of Heathrow. Emily and Jenna met her regularly in Leeds, where they drooled over the gorgeous things in Harvey Nicks and then spent their pocket money in Topshop.

Life-After-Divorce wasn't perfect, but it was OK. And having Auntie O around made all the difference.

'So tell me, what's up?' Auntie O carefully aimed the remote control at the TV and stabbed a finger at the mute button. Behind her, people splashed silently into the water. 'What is it? Boys or school, or both?'

'It's the school play,' Emily told her, feeling the monster whinge bottle-necking inside her. It was all going to come spurting out any second, she could feel it.

'And a boy?'

Why was Emily suddenly thinking about dark eyebrows and a furious glare? What was the new boy, Robert McBride, doing in her head? 'No,' she said firmly. 'It's not a boy. It's just the school play. I've waited years for this and when it's my big chance to act in something totally amazing, they only go and pick *Wuthering Heights* . . . Can you believe it?'

'They haven't . . . ?' said Auntie O, goggle-eyed. 'Really?'

Emily nodded. 'I know. It's hideous. Last year they got to do *The Wizard of Oz*—'

'But that's fabulous news!'

'Huh?' Emily stared at her great-aunt, whose hearing aid must be acting up because this was not the reaction she had been expecting. She wanted genuine outrage and maybe a handful of bourbon biscuits.

'It's totally wild,' sighed Auntie O, staring into nothingness as if she were picturing the main characters running across a windswept moor. 'Such amazing storytelling . . .' She sprang from the sofa and ran eager fingers along the crammed bookshelf, yanking out a battered copy of *Wuthering Heights*. She looked up with sparkling eyes. 'You will be Cathy, won't you? The part was written for you.'

'Um . . . that's the other thing,' muttered Emily. 'Lexie wants to play the lead, and what Lexie wants . . . Lexie usually gets.' She wasn't trying to be dramatic now. This was true.

'Pshaw,' said Auntie O, not fazed in the least.

'You're the star pupil in Drama. Miss Edwards told your father so at the last parents' evening. And I mean this in the nicest possible way, dear, but you even look like Catherine Earnshaw with your mad hairdo.'

Self-consciously, Emily patted her hair. 'But—'

Auntie O shook her head. 'You can be Cathy,' she said, marching the short distance between shelf and sofa, settling herself back against the chenille cushions.

'In Emily Brontë's day it was a struggle for women to be published, and look what she achieved.' As Auntie O launched into a full-blown speech about the difficulties the Brontë sisters faced, Emily knew she was right. Whether she liked the dismal *Wuthering Heights* or not, she couldn't just sit back and let Lexie waltz off with the lead.

Not when the part belonged to Emily.

Chapter Three

'So what's the new boy like?' Jenna asked Emily the next morning. Dad had gone to work early and Auntie O always ate breakfast in her own tiny kitchen, so it was just the two of them.

'Huh?' Emily shrugged. 'I don't know really. I only saw him in Drama. He looked pretty grumpy.' And gorgeous, with dark, dark eyes and one of those brooding, impenetrable expressions they always banged on about in TV costume dramas. But she decided not to share this with Jenna, who would jump to all sorts of stupid conclusions.

Jenna looked up from her cornflakes. 'Grumpy?

You'd get on great then,' she said, her blue-grey eyes gleaming. 'Do you fancy him?'

'Oh, ha ha,' said Emily. Normally she'd be up for a spat, but not today. She'd hardly slept, instead concocting endless plans for winning the part of Cathy. Although there was little point. She'd probably blown it by having such a strop in class. She was so mad with herself.

Clearly disappointed with the lacklustre response, Jenna sighed and went back to patting her cornflakes with the back of her spoon. 'I bet you do fancy him,' she muttered.

Emily lasted two whole seconds before giving in. 'Um ...' she said. 'Is that ... ?' She frowned at Jenna and then smiled. 'Oh, never mind.'

'What?' Jenna was instantly on her guard.

'I thought I saw a curl, that's all,' said Emily, eyes wide.

Jenna shot out of her chair and sprinted to the mirror in the hall. 'Where?' she demanded, just as Emily had known she would. If Jenna's hair were ever left to do its own thing – which it never was – then it would have been a mass of dark curls, just like Emily's. But the difference was that Jenna hated curly hair. If there was even a minor kink, she freaked out.

'Kidding!' Emily called. 'It looks great. Really.' And so did a quick exit right now. Grabbing her bag, she thrust arms into her coat and headed for the back door, reaching it just as her sister reappeared, fuming.

'Bye!' said Emily, slamming the door after her. She set off for school, wondering how Jenna would wreak her revenge this time. Would she hack her Facebook account again? Probably. She must remember to change her password.

Maia was waiting for Emily beside the newsagent's, armed with gossip about the new boy.

'My next-door neighbour's dad's sister-in-law works in the school canteen, right?' said Maia, not even bothering to say hello. 'So this is all totally true.'

Emily decided to ignore the dubious source. 'So, what's the story?' she said. 'I didn't even know he'd started school until I saw him glowering at me in Drama yesterday. Where did he come from?'

They set off down the hill. Emily's toes were jammed right to the front of her school shoes, her knees trembling with the effort of neither sprinting nor slipping onto her behind. Hadn't Dad once told her the slope was something horrendous like one in three down here?

'Well,' Maia announced, 'Robert McBride's from Leeds.'

'And . . . ?' said Emily, unimpressed. Lots of people were from Leeds.

'And,' Maia went on, 'he's a mountain-bike nut.'

'So?' Emily shrugged. Sporty was good, but it was hardly a deal clincher.

'And he's some sort of Goth,' Maia finished triumphantly. 'Out of school, he dresses in black all the time. I don't know about black eyeliner or if he's into that dark, bleak, moody music, but the black gear? Definitely.'

Emily tried to look unmoved. And failed. She did have a bit of a thing about Goths – maybe it was the fact that they always looked as if they needed cheering up – and Maia was totally aware of this. Emily nodded wordlessly, unable to prevent the soppy smile that she just knew was making her look as if her brain had gone on a mini break. Any minute now she would swoon. And on a hill this steep, that wasn't a good idea.

'There's more . . .' whispered Maia. 'He lives with his uncle because his parents are AWOL. Dead or alive, no one knows.' Her eyes lit up. 'Or *maybe* they robbed a bank and they're on the run and Robert's in hiding with the stolen goods and when we least expect it, his mum and dad will screech up to the school in a beat-up old Chevrolet and there'll be a stand-off between them and the police and then we'll all be on the news. That'd be awesome. They might make a film.'

'Eh?' Emily snapped out of her Robert-based reverie and turned to gawp at her best friend. 'What are you on?'

'You love it,' Maia said, looking closely at Emily, who promptly blushed. 'Or . . . do you love *him*?'

What was with everyone this morning? First Jenna and now Maia. Emily felt her cheeks superheat. Actually you couldn't love someone you'd only seen once and had never spoken to. That would be stupid. But . . . there was something about Robert and it wasn't just the Goth factor. Weakly she protested, but neither the outraged expression nor the 'don't talk rubbish!' made any difference. They both knew Maia had scored a direct hit. Emily gave in as gracefully as she could, which wasn't easy when someone was doing a celebratory rumba in her face.

'Just don't tell anyone,' Emily said under her

breath. The ground had started to level out, which meant that they'd nearly reached the foot of the hill, where the grey-brick school nestled. 'He might be the tiniest bit fanciable. But I don't *love* him.'

'Yet,' Maia said, skipping out of reach as Emily swung her school bag in a fast, wide arc. 'You don't love him *yet*.'

Registration was beyond deafening.

Emily covered her ears and tried to block out the noise, but it was no good. She could still hear Lexie, who was quoting large chunks of *Wuthering Heights* to the classroom at large, raising her voice whenever someone tried to speak over her, which meant that anyone else who wanted to be heard had to turn up the volume still further.

This morning's hot topic was the role of Heathcliff and who would play him, but not many of the boys seemed up for it, especially when it was suggested that there was 'soppy stuff' in the book. After a few shouted suggestions, Lexie abandoned her own monologue to announce that as she was going to be Cathy, surely it was up to *her* to decide who would be Heathcliff, and she thought that Daniel would be perfect.

'And it's not just because he's my boyfriend,'

Lexie told the dissenters. 'It's because we have chemistry.'

This was typical of Lexie. Whether it was her boyfriend – she always had a boyfriend – or her five or six best mates, she liked to have a carefully selected posse around at all times. And this included on stage.

Emily gave a short laugh. But all she could think about was keeping a lookout for Robert McBride, who it turned out was going to be in her tutor group as well as her Drama class. Her heart sank a little further each time the classroom door opened to reveal someone who wasn't him. It was only when the new boy shouldered his way angrily into the classroom, just before the bell rang, and there was a collective '*Ooh*' that Emily realised with a sickening jolt she wasn't the only one watching out for him.

Oh.

Apparently there was more than one member of the Unofficial Robert McBride Fan Club. Quite a few more by the looks some girls were giving him.

The door swung wide to reveal Miss Edwards – Emily's form tutor as well as Drama teacher. There was no escaping the woman. 'Robert!' She smiled warmly at him. 'Robert joined us yesterday, everyone, but wasn't here for registration so I couldn't introduce him properly. Some of you may have met him in Drama but the lesson was rather—' Her eyes skimmed the classroom and alighted on Emily, her forehead pinched. 'It was *lively*,' she finished.

Emily swallowed nervously, expecting her to go on. But Miss Edwards looked away and the spectre of the public humiliation passed.

'Everyone, this is Robert McBride,' the teacher said. 'Do please make him welcome. Show him around. Be nice.'

There was a chorus of offers, including a silkily worded one from Lexie that made Daniel sit up and blink.

Emily slumped back in her seat, dispirited. Robert wasn't going to notice her now. She might as well get back to worrying about Cathy Earnshaw because she stood a tiny chance of getting that part. The real-life role of Robert's girlfriend looked about as likely as getting back in Miss Edwards' good books before the auditions.

Robert's fan-base rocketed during the next couple of days. Everyone, apart from Maia who preferred redheads, agreed that he was hot – quite the hottest hottie *ever* to walk the corridors of Upton High School. But when his many admirers began to realise that he was relentlessly unsmiling and seemed determined to ignore everyone, his popularity quickly waned.

'Just look at him,' said Maia over lunch one day. 'How can he be so miserable all the time? I know he's at a new school and everything, but it's not that bad here.'

Emily looked – it was good to have an excuse for once – and tried not to drool. 'Totally miserable,' she agreed. *And completely gorgeous*, she added silently.

Maia scraped back her chair and stood up. 'I'm going to get whatever healthy rubbish is masquerading as pudding. Do you want anything?'

Emily shook her head. As Maia walked away, she looked back at Robert. He was on the other side of the canteen, tearing his way through a hotdog, his dark eyes fixed on a magazine. His body language was shouting *Keep away!* And everyone was – he sat alone. As soon as he finished eating, Robert thrust the magazine into his faded grey rucksack and went outside.

Her chin resting on the heel of one hand, Emily

drummed nervous fingers on her cheek and stared out of the window, tracking Robert to the far corner of the damp school yard. Perhaps he was just lonely, or shy. Maybe he needed someone to talk to. Yes, that was it. She should talk to him. Once she'd plucked up the courage, that was. The teen god was now slumped against a grimy grey stone wall, staring up towards the moors, apparently unaware of the chill wind that sent leaves skittering and repeatedly whipped messy black hair across his tanned face.

Ooh.

Emily's stomach lurched unexpectedly, not unlike the time she ate a whole Scotch bonnet as a dare. And as she watched a soft-focus Robert through the misty glass, she felt a fizzy tingling explode inside her that was like nothing she'd ever felt before.

'*Wow ...*' she whispered as she tried to work out if she was going to pass out, dance, throw up or a combination of all three. Was this what everyone bla-bla-bla'd about in romcoms? Were Jenna and Maia actually right? Was she ... in love?

Filled with a giddy confidence, Emily sprang to her feet. She had to do something right this very minute or she'd lose her nerve. She was going to speak to Robert. And if that went OK, she was going to ask him out. There was the small problem of not knowing what to say – she'd never done this sort of thing before – but surely it couldn't be that difficult. She took a deep breath, pulled on her duffel coat and marched purposefully towards the exit. Her heart drum-rolling in her chest, she pushed open the door . . . and gasped as the cold air slammed into her.

Robert looked up as she approached. She almost bottled it. But something made her go on.

'Er . . . hi,' she began.

Robert stared at her, saying nothing.

'I'm Emily,' she tried again, her voice wobbling nervously. 'So, how do you like it here? Is it very different to where you were before—?'

'You're the girl from Drama, right?' he interrupted. 'The one who had a go at the teacher.'

Emily gave a small nod. She was always getting in trouble for interrupting teachers. When she felt passionately about something, she just couldn't help speaking out. It was unbelievably annoying that Robert had come into her class when she was having one of her outbursts.

'So what do you want?' Robert said.

Emily flinched at the undercurrent of anger in his voice. The lovely warm feeling started to ebb away and fear crept in to replace it. Maybe he sensed this, because his next words were kinder.

'You don't want to bother talking to me,' he said, staring at his scuffed shoes. 'No one else does.'

'Maybe that's because you don't talk to *them*?' Emily pointed out.

Robert shrugged. 'There's no point,' he said, his eyes flicking upwards briefly. 'I won't be staying here long. I never do.'

'Oh.' Emily didn't think she'd ever heard someone sound quite so hopeless. She looked down at the netball markings that striped the concrete and tried to focus on why she was here. The thought of asking him out seemed the most ridiculous thing ever now, but she had to say something. The magazine was poking out of his tattered rucksack. Emily could just make out the word *Singletrack* on the cover. She pointed to it. 'Is that what you were reading earlier? Any good?'

Robert yanked the rucksack onto his shoulder and glared right at her, his eyes dark and stormy. 'Just leave me alone, OK?' he said.

Emily just stared as he stalked away, her eyes welling up. And then she did a mighty sniff and thanked Revlon that she'd gone for the waterproof mascara today.

That boy had issues.

Big issues.

Chapter Four

Emily's run-in with Robert was bad enough; what she hadn't counted on was having an audience. As she stepped back inside the canteen, there was a collective *woop* and her heart sank. How could she have forgotten about the floor-to-ceiling windows that faced the school yard? Had every single person in here watched her be humiliated and rejected? *Oh no*. As Emily stared in growing horror at their gawping faces, she realised that they had.

'Poor Emily,' crowed Lexie, with a beaming smile. 'Did Mr Misery himself give you the brush-off? Oh dear. Not even *he* wants to go out with you.'

'Oh, give it a rest.' Maia put an arm round Emily's shoulders and hurried her away from the crowd that had gathered. At the main doors, she called back, 'Lexie's just fed up with her boyfriends fancying you, Emily.'

'As if,' said Lexie, her eyes narrowing. 'Anyway it was an ex-boyfriend, so it totally doesn't count.'

'Ooooh,' chorused a group of boys and Lexie reddened.

Maia let the doors flap shut behind them and then grinned at Emily. 'That's got her riled,' she said. 'Anyway, what were you *doing* out there? I only went for a kumquat and when I got back you were in the middle of some sort of Mills & Boon drama.'

Emily blushed. 'I thought that maybe I could cheer him up. But, I . . . um . . . didn't,' she finished lamely. She didn't want to go into details right now. She already felt like a total idiot.

'Did he upset you?' asked Maia. 'Only I'll never forgive him if he did.'

'I . . . er . . .' Emily didn't know what was scarier – Robert being mad at her or Maia being mad at Robert. They both did a good line in glaring ferociously. 'Can we just leave it?' she said. 'Please?'

'Fine.' Maia didn't look happy, but she didn't

pry further. 'Come on. Let's go and hide out in the library until this afternoon's lessons. Lexie'll never find us there; I don't think she even knows where it is.'

As they hurried through the empty corridors, Emily decided that next time she spoke to Robert, she'd try not to provoke him again – although quite how she'd stirred him up, she wasn't sure. He'd been sort of OK, before he exploded. But there wasn't going to be a next time, she told herself firmly. She was hurt and humiliated. And she really felt like slapping him for being so rude. But – and this was the weirdest thing – there was a tiny part of her that wanted to hug Robert too, to make him feel better about whatever was messing him up. And this had *nothing* to do with the tiny glimpse she'd had of his dark, soulful eyes. She just figured that people didn't go around acting like wild animals for no reason.

There must be something wrong.

Right?

By the weekend Emily still hadn't worked it out. She and Jenna met up with their mum in Leeds, although Emily held back from discussing Robert with Mum because Jenna was bound to overhear and then it would get so complicated. It had been nearly impossible to convince her sister that nothing was going on after she heard rumours of the incident in the school yard. She wasn't going to start it all off again.

The city was buzzing, window displays already dusted with fake snow and hung with fairy lights. But Emily felt weirdly flat. She wasn't in the mood for Christmas shopping or, actually, *any* kind of shopping. What was wrong with her? Wondering if she was suffering from something terminal, she mooched around H&M, trying to summon up interest in, well, anything. Running her fingers along the top of a clothes rail, she touched a black hoodie that was so not the sort of thing that she usually wore, but would be just right for— *Oh.* Why was she thinking of Robert? She quickly moved to another rail, which shone with sequins. They wouldn't remind her of *him*. Apart from his eyes, that was. *They* glittered when he was really angry.

Argh!

Emily would *not* think about him.

But somehow, Robert was everywhere. The carbon-alloy frame full-suspension mountain bike on sale at only £3000 in the outdoorsy shop reminded her of him; the posters for yet another romantic vampire movie; even the stupid mannequins that stared soulfully out of the front window of Topman. *Unbelievable.* Was she to be rewarded for her extreme kindness towards Robert by being haunted by him for ever?

'Sorry I wasn't around when you got back last night,' Dad said on Monday morning. 'Scouts was manic. Did you have a wicked time?'

'Awesome,' corrected Jenna.

'Wicked,' Dad said, giving her a hug. He looked over to Emily. 'Hey, I met a friend of yours at scouts last night.'

'Huh?' Emily mumbled through a mouthful of cereal, eyes fixed firmly on her *Wuthering Heights* script. Miss Edwards had told them that at the auditions they were all going to be reading a speech by a character called Lockwood, and Emily'd practised it in front of the mirror until she knew it by heart. It had been a good way of getting *him* out of her head.

'Emily?'

She glanced up and realised that Dad was looking at her expectantly. 'Er . . . who was that then?' she asked. 'Which friend, I mean.'

'Robert McBride.'

Emily spat out her cornflakes.

'Ooh, is that the new boy?' asked Jenna, before Emily had recovered enough to speak. 'You've gone all red, Emily. You *do* fancy him, don't you? I knew there was something weird about that thing that happened in the school yard.'

Emily ignored her gleeful sister. 'Dad,' she said, performing a 360° eye-roll, 'Robert and I aren't friends. He's in my class, that's all.' She turned to her sister and smiled. 'And I don't fancy him. But you're the one who keeps talking about him, Jenna, so if *you* do then be my guest. I think you'd make a lovely couple.'

Jenna went scarlet. She grabbed her bag and – pausing briefly to fling a deadly glare over her shoulder – flounced out of the kitchen.

'Bye, Jenna!' Dad looked confused for a second and then he shrugged. 'Anyway I know Robert's uncle – he's that old fellow who runs the computer-repair shop in town. I heard that his nephew was staying and called by to ask if he might be interested in joining the scouts, and he was. Robert came along last night.' Dad pressed his lips together and nodded in a satisfied way. 'What a pleasant lad. Keen mountain-biker, so he tells me. Couldn't shut him up about the magnificent off-roading round here.'

Emily just stared. Had Dad met some sort of alter-ego Robert? A sort of perfect Robert? One with actual manners? 'That's really good, Dad,' she said, privately thinking that *really weird* would be nearer the mark. Talk about inconsistent. How come Robert was mean to her, and pleasant to her dad? What had *Emily* done wrong? Feeling piqued, she got to her feet. 'I'm off to school,' she said. 'I'll be late tonight – it's the auditions for the school play.'

'Coolio,' said Dad. 'Break an arm, won't you?'

'Leg,' muttered Emily, as she left. 'Break a *leg*.'

By the time the Drama students had gathered in the hall after school, it was already getting dark outside. Only the lights over the stage were lit, lending the vast, echoing space a shadowy, spooky feel.

Emily looked around as she waited for Miss Edwards to appear. Lexie was here, blonde hair freshly tonged into a mass of ringlets, eyes big and expectant as she gazed at the empty stage. Emily knew that she was determined to win and her insides churned. To take her mind off her rival, she checked out the rest of the fidgety crowd.

No Robert.

Oh.

After Dad's surprise revelations over breakfast, Emily had been hoping that Robert might have somehow had a complete personality transplant over the weekend. But he hadn't come to school and he wasn't here now. She'd have to wait until tomorrow for him to showcase his new persona. If there was one. She still wasn't convinced she and Dad had met the same Robert. It was a shame he hadn't bothered to come to the auditions though . . . Emily couldn't help thinking that he would have made an amazing Heathcliff to her Cathy.

'I've got some great ideas for the set. It's going to be dark and stormy,' enthused Maia, beside her. She flicked through her thumbed copy of the book and Emily noticed that she'd scribbled notes in all the margins.

It seemed that there was one girl around here who didn't want to be Cathy Earnshaw.

'Hi!' sang Miss Edwards as she rushed through the hall and ran lightly up the wooden stairs to the stage. 'I'm so pleased to see so many of you here.' She smiled beatifically and a little breathlessly. 'And I'll be having words with those of you who aren't . . . um, here.'

A few people frowned uncertainly at this.

'Everyone turn to page one of the script!' the drama teacher went on. 'And if you'll all wait at the back of the hall, I'll see you in turn up on the stage.'

Goose pimples rose unexpectedly on Emily's arms and she nearly spluttered out loud. This wasn't the first time she'd auditioned for a part; she'd been on stage loads of times. She couldn't be scared. *Nooooo.*

She *was* scared.

A tiny squeaking noise came from the hall entrance, neatly interrupting Emily's fear.

'Oh,' said Maia, 'he's decided to turn up.'

Emily saw Robert McBride sliding through the double doors, hunched inside his tatty overcoat. In one hand he held a copy of the *Wuthering Heights* script, but he was shoe-gazing as usual, which made it impossible to gauge anything about his mood. He chose a chair well away from everyone else and huddled behind the sheaf of paper. It didn't *look* as if he'd turned into a 'pleasant lad'.

Even so Emily felt a wave of sympathy. His dark hair wasn't gelled and artfully windswept like the rest of the boys'. It was just an uncombed mess. He didn't seem to care how he looked. She was gazing at the new boy just as he lifted his head and pinioned her to the spot with a cold stare.

'Is he looking at *me*?' Emily whispered to Maia, just to make sure that her imagination hadn't completely run away with her.

'Uh-huh,' said Maia. 'Hey, he's coming over. Maybe he's going to apologise for his outburst in the school yard.' She paused. 'When you pair are an item, can you have a word with him about that frowning? It'll give him wrinkles. He'll need Botox before he's twenty.'

Emily stared in growing amazement as Robert slouched nearer. Maia was quite right – his constant frown wasn't a good look. But he was going to talk to her and that was great.

'Now, don't be shy!' bellowed Miss Edwards.

Robert stopped dead, clearly under the impression that she was talking to him.

'I've put up some screens on the stage today,' the drama teacher went on, 'so no one has to worry about an audience.'

As Emily watched, Robert slunk back to his seat. She puffed out the breath she'd been subconsciously holding. *What had he been going to say?*

Miss Edwards was still talking, her hands

dancing in time to the rhythm of her voice as she went on. 'Now I'm sure you're all dying to get up here and do your *thang*, so to avoid a rugby-scrum situation, we'll be doing the auditions in strict alphabetical order, which means that—'

'I'm first!' said Lexie triumphantly. She detached herself from the group of students now clustered at the back of the hall and strolled across the parquet floor.

Biting her lip nervously, Emily began to thumb through the script, the familiar words refusing to stay still.

This was it.

Two hours, a bag of crisps and a battered and blackened banana later, Emily was still waiting for her turn, wishing her surname began with B and not S and wondering if she'd be back home in time for breakfast.

She stifled a yawn. They were currently at M. For a while it had been entertaining listening to the snippets of dialogue that made it past the screens – Lexie had sounded annoyingly brilliant – but now Emily was bored of doing that too. She'd even done her homework for goodness' sake. But there was an up side: during the yawningly long wait, her nerves had subsided, along with the feeling in her bottom on these hard plastic seats.

Maia had pulled a fast one and managed to volunteer for scenery painting just before the auditions kicked off, so she was gone. There was only a handful of unlucky souls left, Robert among them. Emily thought about going over and asking what he'd wanted, but she was confident that hunched shoulders and a deep frown didn't mean, 'Hey, pull up a chair, why don't you?'

Emily just wanted to get on with *her* audition now. She wanted to dazzle and amaze Miss Edwards. If she could stop yawning that was.

'Robert McBride!' trilled the drama teacher from behind the screens.

At last. The only thing that had kept Emily going for the last hour and a half was seeing what the mysterious Robert would make of the script. She watched transfixed as he unfurled himself from his chair and walked heavily towards the stage as if he were going to the gallows. She found herself sitting slightly forward. This she wanted to hear.

Robert climbed the steps at the side of the stage and vanished from sight. There was total silence ... and then a gorgeously husky voice filled the school hall.

Emily nearly fell off her seat.

'Whoa . . .' she breathed. That didn't sound like Robert. Or did it? Aware that her mouth was hanging open like a panting dog, Emily realised that so far Robert had always spoken in low, angry tones. But the voice beyond the screens rose and fell, gathering speed and then slowing, deepening and quietening into nothingness before roaring forth, and making Emily's stomach flip in a not unpleasant way. Robert was leading-man material. He was *awesome*.

'Next!' sang Miss Edwards. 'Jimmy Nugent, please!'

Was it over already? Emily gawped as Robert slowly descended the steps, eyes firmly fixed on the toes of his boots once more. Looking neither left nor right he headed for the doors, sliding out as quietly as he'd arrived. And Emily knew with total certainty that Heathcliff had just left the room.

Emily was so busy dreaming about Robert and his gorgeous voice that before she knew it, it was the turn of the Ss.

'Emily Sparrow!' called the teacher.

Fear swamped Emily for a second time. She walked towards the stage, trying to control her legs, which were flexing like a couple of bendy straws. She felt clammy too. But at least she knew the words now. She ran through the first couple of lines in her mind.

Er . . . what were they again?

With horror Emily realised that the word-perfect lines had vanished. And so had her confidence. *Bang* went her plans to wow Miss Edwards with her elephant-like memory. All she had to offer now was panic. Overwhelming panic.

As she went up the scuffed wooden stairs, Emily took a couple of deep, yogic breaths. In . . . out . . . in . . . out . . . *Everything is fine*, she told herself. Stuff her elephant memory. She could read from the script, because it was how she *said* the lines that counted. This was her chance to win the part of Cathy. *I can so do this*, she told herself sternly. She had to do this. She had so much to lose if she failed – the lead and the chance to act with Robert. Robert! Why did she keep thinking about him? Why couldn't she get him out of her mind and the words of the script back in? Her palms were suddenly so sweaty that the sheaf of paper turned slippery and she nearly dropped it. Quickly she hugged the precious bundle to her. She was at the top of the steps now. She stepped forward and peered round the screen.

'Miff Fparrow!' mumbled the drama teacher, her cheeks bulging. Hastily she stuffed a purple wrapper into her pocket and swallowed.

Emily stared at the script and took a deep breath.

'Whenever you're ready,' said Miss Edwards.

'*Ihavejustreturnedfromavisittomylandlord*,' gabbled Emily. She stopped. *What?* Something was wrong. That couldn't be her voice . . . It sounded like she was on fast-forward. This wasn't like her at all. Emily was a pro at auditions. She remembered her lines and she spoke them clearly. Sometimes she even rolled her Rs like a *rrr*eal acto*rrr*. *This is just a blip*, Emily told herself firmly.

But now she'd lost her place. Her eyes darted around the trembling script until she found the next line, and then she carried on. But it didn't get any better or any slower. Unbelievably she actually seemed to be speeding up. '*InallEnglandIdonotbelievethatIcouldhavefixedonasituationsocompletelyremovedfromthestirofsociety*,' she squeaked as if she'd just breathed in helium.

Miss Edwards nodded understandingly. 'It's just a touch of stage fright, Emily,' she said. 'Deep breaths, now. If you could say it just a little slower, that would be great.' She looked at her watch.

'*M-r H-e-a-t-h-c-l-i-f-f?*' Emily droned. '*M-r L-o-c-k-w-o-o-d, y-o-u-r n-e-w t-e-n-a-n-t, s-i-r . . .*'

Frowning hard at her script, the Drama teacher held up a hand to stop Emily before massaging small circles into her temples with a thumb and forefinger. She looked up, her smile a little brittle now. 'Come on, Emily. I know you can do this,' she said. 'Forget that you're on stage. Think moors . . . Think wild and wet and windy and misty and cold . . . From the top?'

Suddenly Emily saw Mr Lockwood up on the moors. And it worked. She sprang into character.

Her first words were croaky, but at least they were intelligible. It was a start. Her fingers gripping the script like claws, she read with an increasing fluidity. Now and then she could even lift her eyes from the trembling script; the forgotten lines were coming back to her. Soon the words themselves began to live and breathe and she knew that she wasn't just saying them. She was feeling them too. With astonishment she realised that she liked the words. *Wuthering Heights* and all its wildness and beauty came alive as she spoke. If she'd wanted Cathy's part before, now she had to have it.

'That'll do,' said Miss Edwards, brandishing a pen.

Reluctantly Emily stopped. 'Miss . . .' she ventured, 'I know that I said all that stuff about *Wuthering Heights* the other day, but I'd love to be Cathy, you know.'

The Drama teacher gave a wry smile. 'You and every other girl,' she said. 'You'll find out which part you've got tomorrow.'

'But—'

Miss Edwards gave a small shrug. 'Next!' was all she said.

Chapter Five

On her way home, Emily kept reliving the audition over and over in her head. Had she managed to convince Miss Edwards that she should be Cathy? It was difficult to know, because every time she tried to recapture her audition, all she could hear was Robert McBride's amazing voice.

It was like chocolate for the ears. The good stuff too. None of that milky rubbish. The voice that had caressed her in the school hall was smooth, deep, shot through with bitterness and *so* dark. *Delicious*, in other words.

'Mmm...' she said dreamily, hunching her shoulders against the driving rain. Even the weather

49

seemed to be going all Brontë on her. Not caring that her eyeliner must be halfway down her cheeks, Emily was grinning as she stomped up the last few streets. She couldn't wait to tell everyone at home about the audition and how she hoped she'd won the drama teacher over. She might gloss over the bit where she'd lost her nerve – Jenna would have a field day.

Emily wanted this part so badly now. How she was going to last the long hours between now and tomorrow lunchtime, when the cast list would be announced, she had no idea.

'Dad!' she caterwauled, flinging the back door wide and dancing into the brightly lit kitchen. She performed a few celebratory chorus-line high kicks to the cooker and the dishwasher. 'I'm home!'

'Um . . .' said a voice.

Emily's best jazz hands stilled mid-shake. Slowly she turned round and stared at the one person she knew with complete authority couldn't be sitting at the kitchen table drinking a cup of tea. But somehow was.

'I can't get my legs that high,' observed Robert McBride. In *that* voice. The growly, deep, gorgeously bitter one.

'You?' Emily's arms floated uselessly to her sides

as she wondered vaguely whether she should be phoning the police. Something about him was different. For a moment she couldn't put her finger on it, but then she worked it out: he wasn't scowling. This had the peculiar effect of making him look almost friendly. Dad hadn't been making it up. But why he was here? And where was everyone else?

'Your dad's upstairs,' Robert said, who was apparently telepathic, as well as hot. 'He's talking to your great-aunt.'

Er . . . why, exactly? Emily frowned at the new boy, taking in the creased school uniform, the wild black hair, dark eyes and the non-scowl. With relief she heard a distant thrum of footsteps on stairs and moments later Dad appeared, smiling broadly.

'Hi, sweetheart!' he said. 'How did the audition go? Are we going to see your name in lights before Christmas?'

Uh-oh. Santa jollity meant that something was definitely up. As if the Heathcliff hunk in the kitchen wasn't enough of a clue. Emily wondered if she should be sitting down for this. 'The audition? Oh, it was fine,' she said, trying to keep a lid on her growing unease. 'Dad?' she added. 'Could you please tell me what's going on?'

'Yup.' Dad nodded so fast that he looked like a woodpecker. 'Grab a pew and I'll explain.'

Oh no. He *did* want her to sit down. Had someone died? This must be really bad news.

And as it turned out it was sort of bad news – for Robert. But it was also so bizarre that Emily couldn't take it in at first.

'So let me get this straight,' she said, trying to ignore the heavy-lidded – and ooh, *so* dark – eyes that were fixed on her from the other side of the kitchen table. 'Robert's Uncle Brian is really ill.' She flicked a sympathetic glance in Robert's direction and then had to look away. It was the only way to stay focused. 'And because Robert's only fourteen and all of his other relatives are—'

'Overseas,' said Robert.

'His relatives are overseas,' Emily went on, 'and because social services want to stick him in care . . .'

Dad nodded.

'. . . then you've offered to let him stay here until his uncle's better. And no one knows how long that will be.' She paused. 'Is that everything?'

'Spot on,' Dad said brightly. 'It all kicked off this morning while you were at school. Otherwise I could have told you sooner.'

'I tried to tell you at the auditions,' Robert chipped in helpfully.

'Right,' Emily said slowly. She felt as though all her thoughts were being blown around like snowflakes in a blizzard. *Robert was coming to live here?*

'Anyway,' said Dad, 'Uncle Brian has been whisked off to Sheffield to a specialist unit there, which leaves Robert with no guardian. And seeing as he's new in town, I thought it would be better for him if he wasn't sent off to foster parents miles away, interrupting his schooling a second time. And besides, we've got the room.'

That was another thing. 'Have we?' said Emily, puzzled. The last time she'd looked, the only spare bed was the bottom bunk *in her room*. Surely Dad wasn't suggesting that Robert move in with Emily?

'The Granny Annexe!' said Dad as proudly as if he'd just built it.

Emily felt mild relief.

'I've just been chatting to Auntie O about it. She thinks it's an excellent idea. What we've agreed is that Jenna's going to move into your room. Auntie O is going to move into Jenna's room. And Robert's going to move into the Granny Annexe, so he can have his own space. It's the perfect solution, don't you think?'

The perfect solution? Emily wasn't sure what Jenna would have to say about that. And actually she wasn't sure how much fun it was going to be sharing with a younger sister who was already hell-bent on 'borrowing' everything she touched. But then she saw Dad's nervous smile; his eyes were pleading with her not to make a fuss.

'Sounds cool,' she said. 'Really.'

'Hey, you and Robert can practise your lines together for the school play,' said her dad. 'Won't that be *great*?' By now his face was deliriously happy; he was never more cheerful than when he could help out.

'Yeah,' said Emily. And then a spotlight switched on in her brain and she saw with dazzling clarity that this was just what she and Robert needed. Cosy evenings spent huddled around the *Wuthering Heights* script, getting to know him, finding out about his mysterious past . . . She'd be Cathy. He'd be Heathcliff.

'Anyway, how did this chap do?' asked Dad, changing the subject as clumsily as he clapped Robert on the back. 'At the audition, I mean. He tells me that he thinks he did OK.'

'Yeah,' Emily said again. *OK* was one way of putting it. *Totally divine* was another. Aware that a gooey smile was decorating her face, but incapable of doing anything about it, she returned briefly to her fabulous daydream of them helping each other with their lines. Moving Robert in was Dad's best idea ever. She couldn't think about anything else for now.

The back door banged shut.

'Hi, Jenna!' called Dad. 'How was the disco?'

'Ballet,' said Jenna, looking suspicious. Her eyes flicked in Robert's direction. 'Why's *he* here? What's going on?'

Quickly Dad recapped, speeding up when he got to the part about Jenna moving into the bottom bunk. Emily saw her sister flinch and she sympathised – the thought of Jenna invading her personal space was making her twitch – but there was the inarguable bonus that Emily would be getting to know the new boy away from the staring eyes of everyone at school.

'Fine,' said Jenna, once Dad had finished. White-lipped and trembling, she glared at Robert, who was staring fixedly into his cup as if he'd suddenly learned how to read fortunes. 'I get it.' She left the room.

Dad looked anxiously at Emily. 'Is she OK, do you think?' he asked.

'Yeah,' Emily replied, not because Jenna was fine – she clearly wasn't – but because this was what she knew Dad wanted to hear. Her father smiled with relief. Emily knew Jenna *would* be fine. She'd go and check on her later, after she'd hidden her make-up. 'So,' Emily said, smiling at Robert, 'have you got much gear?'

Robert smiled, actually *smiled*. 'Just a bit,' he said.

Emily couldn't help grinning back. He was cheering up already and she was beyond thrilled. No one else got the chance to be this close to their future boyfriend. Imagine bypassing embarrassing dates and hours spent sitting rigid in the cinema, wondering if he was going to make a move. They'd have *none* of that mucking about. This whole living-under-the-same-roof thing was going to be *so* cool. Jenna would soon get her head round the new living arrangements. Emily'd make her younger sister feel right at home in her room. She could think of at least one drawer that Jenna could use. But right now Emily wanted to get to know the new lodger.

*

Later Emily lay on the prized top bunk, so much stuff ricocheting inside her head that it felt like a squash court in there. Robert – and a small holdall and two mountain bikes and more tools than the local hardware shop – had officially arrived. He was so close right now, and she couldn't resist a silent *yes!* of excitement at the thought.

A gentle snoring drifted up from beneath her, a reminder that Jenna was even closer than Robert and also that she, and not Emily, was asleep. When Emily had asked her sister what was wrong, Jenna had shrugged and pulled the weirdest face. 'Are we not enough for Dad?' she'd said. 'Why does he have to move *him* in?'

Moonlight illuminated the edge of the softly billowing curtains. And then it was dark again. The windows were shut, but they were the old wooden sash type and they rattled when the wind blew, as it did now, uneven gusts howling across the moors and swirling noisily around anything in their path. Quietly, so as not to wake Jenna, Emily crept down the wooden ladder and padded to the window. She slid between the curtains and let them close behind so that she was alone with the darkness.

For a few seconds she couldn't see much at all, just the shadowy outline of an oak tree beyond the garden. And then clouds fled away from the curved moon and the vast moor was revealed. Entirely robbed of colour, it was an eerie black-and-white-movie set with every shade of grey in between. A queue of clouds floated across the night sky, each one covering the moon and briefly plunging everything into blackness, before it moved on and the wild moor shone once more. Clusters of trees were bunched here and there. Emily watched as the wind cut through the heather like an invisible comb, parting it this way and that. In the distance she saw a house, set on the highest part of the moor. She couldn't remember who lived there. She shivered. It must be a lonely existence.

Haworth, where the Brontës had spent their short lives, was just across the moors; which meant that she and they must have gazed on almost the same savagely beautiful view.

For the first time since the crushing disappointment she'd felt when Miss Edwards had chosen this year's play, Emily began to feel just the tiniest bit optimistic about the story of *Wuthering Heights*. Maybe, just maybe, Robert was the magic ingredient in Emily Brontë's mad love story that would save the school play from being a total disaster.

As she watched, a mass of clouds stormed towards the moon, covering it swiftly and completely. Not a glimpse of the moor remained. Emily's eyelids grew heavy as tiredness rushed towards her at last. With a yawn, she dodged the curtains and climbed back to the top bunk.

And then, at last, she slept.

Chapter Six

Overnight the wind grew wilder. By morning strong gusts were bending the trees so far over that they stooped like pensioners. It was raining so hard that Dad made the rare move of offering Emily, Jenna and Robert a lift to school in his ancient Land Rover.

'Dad never takes us to school,' muttered Jenna. 'This is all for *his* benefit.' But Emily's sister – who was refusing to call Robert by his name – changed her mind when she opened the back door.

It was seriously wild out there.

'Hey, at least the car's getting a wash, eh?' Dad said, once they were all inside the 4x4, considerably wetter than they'd been before the short dash from the house.

Jenna ignored him and plugged herself into her pink DS.

'Um . . . yeah,' said Robert, after a brief pause.

Emily wanted to join in but she felt curiously shy. Dad started up the 4x4 and pointed it into the first storm of the autumn. With a great judder they set off, rivulets of water streaming down the windscreen as the rain pounded even harder.

'What's that pipe for?' Robert asked, pointing to a tube sticking out of the Land Rover.

Dad seemed delighted that someone was interested in his pride and joy. 'It's in case we go underwater,' he said. 'It's a raised air intake, otherwise known as a snorkel. It allows air to travel to the engine so that it doesn't conk out in mega-wet driving conditions. Cool, huh?'

'Cool,' agreed Robert, who was now examining the dashboard, reverently running his fingers in and out of every dusty cavity.

Emily had only ever asked one car-related question: Where's the MP3 player? The answer had been so ridiculous that she'd never asked another. The Land Rover didn't even have a radio. This was a driver's car, Dad had explained. It was for negotiating mountain tracks and storming through raging torrents. It wasn't a portable disco.

'What about the torque?' asked Robert, who clearly knew a lot more about cars.

'Stuff the torque. I wish they'd stop *talking*,' muttered Jenna, not lifting her eyes from the DS. 'This male bonding is doing my head in.'

Emily elbowed her sister. 'Dad's just making him feel at home,' she whispered. In a louder voice, she said, 'Can you give me a lift to Maia's this evening, Dad?' This was partly to remind Robert that she was here, but mostly because she did actually want to go to Maia's house. Emily needed to tell her everything. And she didn't want to have to do it in the girls' toilets.

'I'm sorry, love,' Dad replied, his eyes searching for hers in the rear-view mirror. He flashed an apologetic look. 'I told Robert that I'd take him to the bike shop before scouts. Can't you Skype or something?'

'Er, no . . .' said Emily. 'Maia doesn't have a webcam.' But Dad didn't seem to hear.

Jenna lifted her head and turned to Emily. 'I bet he's *always* wanted a son,' she whispered, stabbing a finger towards the back of Dad's seat. 'Now he's got one.'

Emily didn't bother replying.

Sometimes her sister could be *so* childish.

The great debriefing ended up happening in the girls' toilets after all. Emily told Maia everything. Her best friend was speechless – for the three seconds that it took her to absorb the news – and then she wasn't. She was *really* loud. Emily began to wish that she'd at least warned her by text the night before. Or worn ear defenders. Now Maia was staring at Emily as if she'd just announced something totally insane. Which, Emily had to admit, she sort of had. Strange boys didn't move in every day of the week around here.

'Robert McBride?' shrieked Maia. 'The boy who dumped you in front of the whole school is living in your house?'

'Are you aware that you're exceeding safe levels for sound?' Emily shouted back. 'And he didn't dump me, actually,' she said, more quietly. 'He could only have done that if he was my boyfriend.'

'Robert McBride's your boyfriend?' asked a Year Eight girl, peering out of one of the cubicles. 'The miserable one? You've *moved in* with him—?'

'Out!' said Maia, pointing helpfully towards the exit.

The girl swiped her hands under a dripping tap and left, but not without giving Emily a strange look.

'Cheers,' Emily said, narrowing her eyes at Maia. 'The whole school is going to think that my life has turned into a Christmas episode of EastEnders.'

Maia nodded sympathetically. 'True.'

'You're not supposed to agree with me,' said Emily. Quickly she did what she wished she'd done five minutes earlier, and checked under the remaining cubicle doors before adding, 'I'm a little freaked out by it. He's gorgeous. And he's living in my house. I'll see him every day. Is that or is that not weird?'

'Weird.' Maia nodded. 'Imagine a boy in your bathroom . . . Gross.'

'He has his *own* bathroom,' said Emily, slowly and clearly. Was Maia concentrating at all here? She was beginning to wish that she'd brought her own subtitles. 'He's in the Granny Annexe, remember?'

The door creaked open and a gaggle of Year Sevens barged in.

'They're all full,' said Maia, brandishing her fiercest frown like a deadly weapon. Wisely the girls opted against checking this statement for truth, and U-turned instead. Once the door had sucked shut behind them, Maia went on. 'I'm sure that's illegal. A strange boy living in your house, I mean. Aren't there laws against that sort of thing?'

'I'm sure it's all above board,' said Emily. 'Dad knows all about it because of his job. He did all the paperwork yesterday and then took Robert to get his stuff last night. He's filled the garage, you know. You should see the amount of mountain-bike junk he's rammed inside. Two bikes and spare wheels and—'

'Did you find out what's happened to his parents? Are they missionaries?' asked Maia, her eyes wide. 'I bet they are. Or what if they're totally loaded and they want their son to have a taste of real life? Or maybe' – at this, her eyes shone – 'he's a foreign prince and he's taking part in that TV series where they search for their future wife on a council estate. Imagine that ... You might be on TV. You might be his princess.'

'Stop!' Snorting with laughter, Emily caught Maia by the shoulders and pushed her gently towards the door.

By Physics, everyone was talking about Robert moving in with Emily. It was officially the best gossip in years, and way more interesting than the electromagnetic spectrum.

Emily kept her head down, steadfastly ignoring the jabbing elbows of her neighbours and the screwed-up notes that kept skittering across her desk. She'd been so sure that they were all going to make fun and she was right.

'What's got into everyone this morning?' wailed Mr Elton, who wasn't known for his classroom-discipline skills. He stared pitifully at them all through bulbous lenses; whichever way he turned, his eyes ballooned and shrank alarmingly, making him look like a cartoon monster.

'I think, sir, that it's probably because of *Wuthering Heights*,' replied Robert.

There was a collective gasp and then a stunned silence as everyone swivelled their heads until they were facing the new boy. He'd spoken! Because the rest of the class was looking that way, Emily decided it was fairly safe to do the same and – *oh!* – those were long eyelashes. She could see them from here.

'And why's that?' asked Mr Elton.

Robert rocked back in his chair. 'Because they're announcing the cast list at midday?' He arched one arrogant eyebrow at the teacher, which had the peculiar effect of making him look slightly lopsided, but at the same time totally hot.

Thump! The front legs of Robert's chair landed back on the floor again, and everyone jumped.

Abruptly all the pupils seemed to remember that they had vocal cords and a fixed opinion about who should get which part, and the classroom dissolved into a fierce debate that lasted the entire lesson and meant that no one could indulge in idle rumour-mongering about Robert McBride's new lodgings, for which Emily was truly grateful.

After Physics came PE, when it was impossible for anyone to gossip. The mud-splattered cross-country run also made it difficult to breathe. Beetroot-faced but otherwise unscathed, Emily made it to midday, when she joined the rest of the Drama students stampeding towards the entrance hall. By now she wanted to be Cathy Earnshaw so badly that a hard, longing knot of desire had formed in her chest.

Was she going to be Robert's leading lady?

'I'm so nervous . . .' Emily whispered to Maia, who had come along for moral support. 'What if I don't get the part?' Then an equally terrifying thought occurred to her. 'What if I *do*? What if I get stage fright again?'

'Eh?' Maia said. 'I thought you wanted to be an actress?'

'*Her*, an actress?' Lexie butted in. 'Don't make me laugh.' And then, for the benefit of everyone in the vicinity, she laughed loudly anyway. 'She couldn't act surprised if a balloon popped in her face.'

Emily clamped her front teeth on her bottom lip to stop it from trembling. She didn't trust herself enough to speak. But there was no need to worry about repelling Lexie's next jibe because the other girl had already moved on. Pied-Piper-like, she led the crowd towards the notice board and there was silence as her eyes and a dozen others' darted about like pinballs.

'It's not here,' said Lexie, her pretty face screwed into an angry scowl. 'This is ridiculous—'

'Here she is!' called Maia.

Miss Edwards emerged from the headteacher's office, in her hand the list that everyone wanted to see. She fought her way through the crowd and pinned the single sheet of paper securely to the top of the notice board. Then she broke free of the mob and ran – actually ran – down the corridor, towards the safety of the staff room. Before the sound of her heels had faded, the cast list was ripped down and seconds later it was firmly in Lexie's possession. Triumphantly she waved it aloft and then peered closely.

In spite of herself, and her almost pathological urge to look as if she wasn't bothered, Emily leaned forward a little.

So did everyone else.

'Mr Earnshaw is . . . Jason Bell!' announced Lexie.

Emily decided that this was a promising start. Jason was officially a nice lad. He'd be great as Cathy's father.

'Mrs Earnshaw . . . Hindley Earnshaw . . .' Lexie ran her index finger down the list, apparently bored of the announcement process already, and skimmed the names until she found one she liked the look of. Her finger stopped dead. Slowly she lifted her head until she was looking right at Emily, her blue eyes shining with triumph. 'Guess what?' Lexie said. 'Catherine Earnshaw is . . . *me*!'

Emily felt as if she'd been punched.

'Fix,' muttered Maia.

If Lexie heard her, she didn't let on. She beamed at everyone in turn, Emily last of all. 'I'm so sorry,' she said. 'How disappointing for you. But the best woman won, don't you think?'

Emily said nothing. She couldn't take it in. Lexie had won the part, not her? This wasn't in the script. It was only Maia's reassuring arm round her shoulders that stopped her from crying right there and then.

'Now . . .' said Lexie, returning her attention to the cast list. She scanned the sheet of paper with grim intent. 'Where's my Heathcliff?'

Oh, no.

Emily gritted her teeth, bracing herself. *Nooooo.* Not that as well.

'Here we are,' said Lexie. 'Heathcliff.' She seemed to be having difficulty speaking. 'Heathcliff . . . is . . . Robert McBride?' she said, screwing her eyes up as she peered more closely at the piece of paper. 'Robert McBride? That miserable sod?'

Lexie's words left-hooked Emily's jaw and she flinched on Robert's behalf. Then her eyes skimmed the crowd to see if he was there. She didn't spot him at first. And then she glanced across the entrance hall and saw that Robert was leaning nonchalantly against the wall. He didn't look in the least bit upset that Lexie had dissed him so publicly. If anything, he looked amused.

'I can't act with Robert,' Lexie muttered, half to herself now. 'We don't have chemistry, not like me and Daniel. I'm going to tell Miss Edwards so.' Furiously she crumpled the cast list and hurled it at the wall, before stomping off in the direction of the staff room.

Several Year Tens dived for the ball of paper and there was a brief scrum as it was shunted around the floor. Eventually Sam won possession and smoothed it out on his knee before announcing the rest of the names in a deep voice.

'Hey, he's not bad,' said Maia. Then she hurriedly added, 'Nice diction, I mean. He's a good actor. I don't fancy him.'

Clearly Miss Edwards agreed, because he'd been cast as Hareton Earnshaw, who Miss Edwards had told them was Hindley's beleaguered son. Sam gave a small, modest smile before carrying on with the cast list.

Emily grew increasingly anxious. Devastated to be missing out on the role of Cathy, the spectre of something much worse loomed. Where was she? Had she been so bad in her audition that Miss Edwards hadn't chosen her to play anyone? By now Emily didn't even mind who she was playing, just as long as she was *in* the play—

'And Nelly Dean is . . . Emily Sparrow!' Sam finished with a flourish. He flicked back his surfer hairdo and carefully pinned the battered cast list back on the notice board.

'Phew!' Emily blew out the breath she'd been subconsciously holding. She was in! And then she did a double-take. 'Nelly Dean . . . ?' she asked Sam, just to make sure. Because it sounded horribly like she'd be playing the interfering busybody who seemed to spend most of the play just getting in the way of the important characters, and *not* kissing Robert . . . um, Heathcliff.

'Nelly Dean, the servant woman.' Sam smiled. 'Congratulations! She's in nearly every scene, I think. You'll be on the stage *loads*. It's a big part.'

'Mmm.' That didn't really help. Emily glanced furtively left and right, wondering what Robert thought. Maybe he'd be gutted not to be co-starring with her, and then she'd know that he felt something for her. But she quickly saw that he wasn't here. He must have left directly after Heathcliff had been revealed, which meant that he hadn't even stayed to find out which part she was playing. She swallowed a sob. She felt even more humiliated and hurt. He was living in her house, but he didn't care about her at all.

The announcements over, the crowd began to break up, small groups drifting in the direction of the canteen. Emily allowed herself to be carried along by the hungry tide.

'Hey, it's not so bad,' said Maia, giving her a squeeze.

'Isn't it?' Emily asked, unable to keep the whine out of her voice. She knew that she sounded pathetic, but this was terrible. She was going to be watching another girl playing the part she wanted . . . snogging the boy she wanted . . . in a play based on *Wuthering Heights*, which she totally hadn't wanted, but was having to put up with.

'Yeah . . .' said Maia, nodding sagely. 'Actually ignore what I said. It's a disaster, darling.'

Emily stuck her tongue out at Maia. Then she chased her so-called best friend down the corridor while swinging a school bag at her head.

It was only a play.

Chapter Seven

Supergluing on a brave face was easy; keeping it there was hard.

Robert wasn't even around at lunch time. Reappearing just as afternoon lessons were about to begin, he answered anyone who dared to congratulate him on his Heathcliff role with a furious glare, so Emily didn't join in. Besides he still hadn't said a single word to Emily about *her* part, which was almost as upsetting as losing out on the lead role to the school's resident prima donna.

Last night he'd been almost charming. Today? *Nada.* As for working out what was wrong with him ... Who even cared? Not Emily. Besides, she had troubles of her own. She hadn't got the star part and Auntie O and Dad would be disappointed. Not to mention having to watch Lexie being Cathy instead of her. That was the worst bit of all.

By the final bell Emily's fixed grin was wavering, and she ran for it, reaching home just as the street lamps were beginning to glow. Jenna was out at some new tap-dancing class, so she closed her bedroom door, alone at last, and the brave face came spectacularly unstuck.

Emily sank down into a melodramatic heap on the floor and howled.

'It's not f-f-fair,' she sobbed to one of Jenna's discarded Barbie dolls. 'Who's going to notice the dull old s-servant in the corner . . . ?' She'd been going over and over it *all day*. It was her fault, mostly. If Emily hadn't succumbed to stage fright, she was almost positive that she'd be Cathy now. But it was Robert's fault too – him and his stupid, husky voice. *He'd* distracted her completely and ruined the first few lines of her audition.

There was a quiet tap at the door.

Oh, no. Jenna was back already. Emily put her head in her hands and sobbed harder. The last thing she wanted was to be interrupted. Jenna would just poke fun. Or start whingeing about something pointless, like how Robert had sat in the front seat that morning when he wasn't even a blood relative. And Emily so wasn't in the mood. Then she remembered that Jenna never knocked.

'Is anything wrong, darling?' warbled a sing-song voice.

'Auntie O?' *Oops*. Emily must have been very loud if her great-aunt had heard. She was practically deaf. Gulping back tears, she dragged her sleeve across her nose and did an almighty sniff before replying, 'I'm fine!'

The handle twisted, the door creaked open, and Auntie O crept into the room, eyes twinkling. In her hand was a foil-wrapped slab of Green & Black's.

Emily managed a watery smile. 'Do you need any help with that . . . ?'

'I do,' Auntie O said firmly, 'can't stand the stuff. Give me a tin of Quality Street any day.'

'*Ew*,' said Emily. Then she ripped open the packet and snapped off three squares, popping them into her mouth in one go, sighing as the bitter-sweetness flowed through her. It was uncanny how her great-aunt always got it right. Extreme nice-ness or pull-yourself-togetherness and she'd be in floods again by now. Instead, she was feeling marginally less devastated already.

'Come on, then,' said Auntie O, sitting down on the bottom bunk. 'Tell me all about it.'

Because the entire inside of Emily's mouth was coated with chocolate, she went for the abridged version. 'So now I'm not Cathy like you wanted me to be, and that spoilt brat Lexie is, and she's going to gloat about it for ever,' she finished, hardly able to believe the relief she felt at off-loading everything. Nearly everything. She hadn't told Auntie O about her stupid crush on Robert, or the fact that he hadn't comforted her after the announcement. 'How totally rubbish is that?'

'Never mind, dear. Now you can be a fabulous Nelly Dean instead.'

Emily pulled a face. 'Really?'

'Why don't you read the script?' said Auntie O. 'Properly, this time. All the way through.' She got to her feet and stroked Emily's hair. 'You might change your mind.'

Emily rolled her eyes, but didn't argue. If nothing else, staying in her room for a while might give her face a chance to return to its normal hue.

The door clicked shut.

She picked up the script . . .

. . . and two hours later Emily put it down, sighed and stretched lazily.

Miss Edwards must have worked wonders, because this play version wasn't bad. Tragic? Yes. There weren't a lot of laughs. But it wasn't dull at all – it was passionate and raw. And Nelly Dean did manage to get in on just about every scene – and if she wasn't in it, she was gossiping about it to someone else – so if there were any talent scouts from the Royal Shakespeare Company in the audience, then she was going to be right in their faces for the whole play.

Result.

The following morning the best October could rustle up was a stiff breeze and steel-grey skies, which meant that when Jenna asked if they'd be getting a ride to school again, Dad refused point-blank and told her not to be so lily-livered.

'Typical,' Jenna muttered into her cereal bowl. 'Bet if *he* asked, Dad would say yes.'

'Eh?' said Emily. Then she clicked. 'Oh . . . Robert.'

'Yeah,' Jenna whispered. 'Did you know Dad was helping him for ages with his lines last night for your stupid play? He was meant to be testing me on my French verbs but I had to get Auntie O to help me because he was in the Granny Annexe with his precious new son.'

'Oh.' Emily wasn't sure how she felt about that. Nobody had offered to help with her lines, but to be honest she hadn't even thought about learning them yet. Miss Edwards had said it was just a read-through of the first scene this afternoon so she hadn't worried about it too much. Maybe she should have been more prepared, or maybe Robert was just really keen. She didn't feel jealous though. She knew Dad was just trying to help Robert – he was like that. Jenna was blowing it all out of proportion.

Dad folded up his newspaper and picked up his empty mug. 'Why don't you pair hang on for the new lodger?' he said. 'You could walk to school together.'

Jenna scowled. 'Do I *have* to?'

'Well, not if you don't want to,' Dad replied, plucking the shiny hexagonal coffee pot from the hob and pouring out the thick, tarry gloop that he loved.

'Good,' said Jenna, and promptly left.

'Emily?' asked Dad.

Nervous excitement pounded inside Emily's chest. She hadn't forgiven Robert for avoiding her yesterday, and who knew which Robert it would be this morning? Miserable Robert or Charming Robert? With a pseudo-casual shrug, she helped herself to another slice of toast. 'OK.'

Robert appeared seconds later, looking as if he'd slept in his uniform.

'Emily wondered if you'd like to walk to school with her,' said Dad.

'No, I ... erm ...' Emily's words faded as Robert looked in her direction. 'I'm going now, if you're ready,' she said.

'Yeah ... right.' Grabbing a slice of toast and quickly smearing it with – *eww* – Marmite, he turned to face Emily and flashed her a grin so totally disarming that it made her knees tremble.

Charming Robert, definitely.

'Ready?' he said.

Emily managed a brief nod. Suddenly, she *so* was.

Dad grinned at her. 'Thanks, love,' he mouthed.

As they set off *together*, Emily was as warm as the toast she'd just eaten. Personalised central heating must be a by-product of having a crush on someone. On a cold, autumn day, it made the pillar-box cheeks and the total tongue-tied-ness almost worth it.

For the first street and two corners, neither of them spoke. The only sound came from traffic growling in a low gear and the rhythmic thudding of their school shoes. Emily wondered if he must be irked to have her foisted on him, but was too polite to say so.

They paused on the edge of the pavement and, in looking left and right, their eyes made contact. Emily beamed nervously; Robert did a grimace-grin. After a fraction of a second, they looked away and crossed over, carrying on down the hill.

The silence was growing uncomfortable now.

Her heart going as fast as one of Jenna's favourite hip hop tracks, Emily went for it. 'So, I'm a bit hacked off at being Nelly D—'

'Hey, I can't believe—'

They both spoke at exactly the same time . . . stopped . . . apologised . . . interrupted each other again . . . and finally laughed. The ice was broken and Emily felt herself relax, just a bit. 'What were you going to say?' she asked.

'I . . . um . . . can't believe you're not going to be Cathy,' mumbled Robert. 'The drama teacher's a muppet for not choosing you.'

Emily was so busy being gobsmacked that she walked straight into a streetlamp. Bouncing off it with as much grace as possible – which was very little – she tried to ignore what was going to be a massive bruise on her shoulder. This was exactly what she'd imagined him saying the day before. She really wished that she could believe him. 'But-but-but you weren't there for my audition,' she said. 'How do you know?'

His cheeks reddened.

Emily felt a quiet thrill run through her. This must be a sign that he actually felt something for her. She could hardly wait for the next revelation. *He knew in his heart of hearts that she was a brilliant actress,* maybe? *All he had to do was look at her and he saw Cathy?* Or – and this was the one she really wanted him to say – *There was such a connection between them in real life that recreating it on stage would be a dream come true for him.* Fireworks began to explode inside her. This was awesome.

Robert shrugged. 'It was just the way you kicked off in Drama when you heard that we'd be doing *Wuthering Heights*,' he said. 'This Cathy is quite a handful, so I figured you'd be good at being her.'

The fireworks fizzled out. 'Oh,' said Emily. Was

this meant to impress her? That she was a handful like the wild, passionate, spoilt Cathy? Great.

'What I mean is that you stood up for yourself like her, like Cathy.' Robert now seemed to be speaking to his thumbnail, which he proceeded to chew with fierce determination.

Emily frowned, hard. But she still couldn't work it out. What did he *mean*? Was a handful of a girl, who was good at standing up for herself, actually a good thing?

'Anyway, catch you later,' Robert said.

'What?' said Emily, dragged forcibly from her mixed-up thoughts by this abrupt farewell. 'Where are you going?' She'd been just about to pin him down like a top interviewer with the most erudite question in the history of For Ever: *Did he like her or not?* He couldn't just take off now. She wasn't finished.

'Erm . . . school?' he replied. 'Where are *you* going?'

Oh.

'We're here,' she said, feeling stupid.

He nodded. 'See ya.'

Then he was gone, and Emily was left with the unsettling feeling that instead of knowing more about Robert, she somehow knew less. And now she had just a few hours to get her head straight before he had a chance of scrambling it again at the first rehearsal.

Chapter Eight

Before Emily was anywhere near ready to face Robert on stage, it was dusk and she was making her way along rapidly emptying corridors towards the school hall. She dragged her feet, but it made no difference. Too soon she was standing in front of the heavy wooden doors, wondering how it was possible to feel such a mixture of feverish excitement and nerves. A strange, high-pitched giggle escaped her. Oh no. Now she was turning into the village idiot too.

'Welcome!' It was Miss Edwards, looking maybe eighty per cent as scary as usual, which Emily figured was a start. 'We're nearly all here,' said the drama teacher. 'Come and join the others.'

Relaxing slightly, Emily peered inside. Like last time only a few of the lights directly over the stage were lit. This gave the school hall a slightly spooky feel and did absolutely nothing to quell her nerves. Emily knew that Maia was relieved not to be part of the cast, but her not being here felt plain weird. They usually did everything together. Now it was just Emily. As she walked in, she looked at the cavernous parquet floor that would be filled with seats, rows and rows of seats. And an audience, with her own family in it. She swallowed and wished she hadn't had the jam roly-poly for pudding. She had a horrible feeling that it was going to make a reappearance.

Keeping her head down, she moved soundlessly to the area directly in front of the stage where the rest of the students were sitting. There were fifteen or so of them here, artfully arranged on the school's hard plastic chairs, slouching as low as they could without actually sliding off. She spotted Robert's ducked head right away. He was gripping his tatty script with stiff fingers and staring so hard at the first page that it looked in danger of combusting any second.

Robert's mood had flipped *again*. The boy she'd walked to school with was gone. And she wasn't going near this one in case he lost his rag like the time in the school yard.

Emily slid into the nearest seat, realising too late that she was sitting next to Lexie. The other girl flicked her a disdainful glance and got back to entwining her fingers with Daniel's. *Urgh*. They'd better not keep that up or Emily really was going to barf.

'Look, Daniel,' Lexie said sweetly, 'it's one of the extras. There must be a crowd scene for her to *get lost* in.'

'Don't worry, Lexie,' Emily replied, 'I'm sure most of the cast will be hidden behind your big head anyway.'

Just as Lexie was about to snipe back, Miss Edwards approached the front of the hall and ran lightly up the steps that led to the stage. 'Act one, scene one!' she sang, checking her script. 'That means I'd like Lockwood, Heathcliff, Joseph, Hareton, Catherine Heathcliff and . . . yes, Nelly Dean, on stage.' The drama teacher was nearly Riverdancing with excitement.

Nelly Dean? Already? Emily's jam roly-poly did a back flip. All around students were scraping back their chairs and moving towards the stage, which seemed to be at least a metre higher than it had been a few minutes ago. Was it even safe to be acting so high up? What if she got vertigo? She felt sick.

'Let's get this party started,' said Lexie, leading the way up the stage steps.

Miss Edwards smiled kindly. 'I'm delighted that you're so keen, Lexie, but you're not actually in this scene.'

There was a ripple of laughter from the other students.

'Duh . . .' said Lexie. She pointed to the script. 'It says there, miss. Catherine. That's me.'

'You're Catherine *Earnshaw*,' said the drama teacher patiently, 'who becomes Catherine *Linton*. Catherine *Heathcliff*, who's in this scene, is . . . ah, there you are, Ruby. Come on up.'

Sheepishly, Ruby hurried up the stairs.

Lexie exited stage left, muttering, 'Why does everyone have the same name in this stupid book?'

With all eyes on Lexie, Emily decided that now was the perfect moment to slip onto the stage unnoticed. Head down, she dodged her way through the small crowd . . . and walked *slap-bang* into *Robert Heathcliff*. No . . . *Robert McBride*. Arghhh. She was as bad as Lexie.

Robert glared at Emily and she flinched.

Uh-oh. Clearly Miserable Robert was back and in full-on glower mode too.

'After you,' he snarled.

Blushing furiously, she went first.

'I agree that all the names are a little confusing to begin with,' Miss Edwards was saying, 'and this is why I've put a handy family tree on the last page of the script. And don't worry, there are no spoilers,' she added. 'As you'll all know by now, *Wuthering Heights* is very much told in flashback, so we get to know the set-up quite early on. The story is how we get there. And what happens to all of the characters in the end, of course.'

There was a frantic rustling of paper. Obviously Emily was the only one who'd read the whole thing.

They kicked off with a read-through of the first scene, and once Miss Edwards had told them not to worry too much about following the stage directions – it was fiendishly difficult to read and do stuff at the same time – Emily forgot she was nervous and actually started to enjoy herself.

The real surprise was Robert. While the rest of them repeatedly stumbled over their lines, dissolving into laughter every time they got it wrong, he was word perfect. Emily noticed that he didn't even look at his script. The practice with Dad last night must have really helped. Even more amazingly, when he spoke, the words were infused with emotion.

He wasn't reading it; he was acting it.

He was Heathcliff.

And he was fabulous.

Chapter Nine

Emily braced herself, tugged and '*Ow!*' Triumph-antly she held her tweezers aloft. 'Got one.'

It was Saturday, at last, and Emily and Maia were lounging on her bunk. Maia was expertly daubing her toenails with Urban Sunset – a weird yellowy black that Emily had politely turned down.

Jenna was elsewhere, as she seemed to be most of the time at the moment. She said she was sick of sharing a room, but not as sick as she was of Robert, who she had nicknamed *The Usurper*, claiming that he was only here to steal Dad's affec-tions. And probably the family silver, if they'd had any. Poor Robert was on the receiving end of most of her vitriol.

Emily tried her best to deflect the more poisonous jibes that Jenna flung in his direction, but she soon saw that Robert didn't seem that bothered. Or was very good at being polite. Over the last couple of days, he'd settled into a comfortable routine of being Charming Robert at home, while saving his moody alter ego for school. Emily didn't get it, but at least she knew roughly what to expect.

'How's it going?' Maia asked.

'My art homework, you mean?' asked Emily.

'That? Of course not,' said Maia. 'It only took me five minutes. I painted it black and called it *"Despair"*. Cool, huh?'

'Genius,' said Emily. 'I wish I'd thought of it.'

'I was inspired by your resident Goth.'

Emily sighed. 'He's not my Goth. He's not *my* anything.'

'Good,' said Maia. Seeing Emily's shocked face, she protested, 'I haven't forgiven him for being so mean to you in the school yard yet.' She paused to admire her toenails that now looked as if she'd dipped them in crude oil, and then turned to stare at Emily, narrowing her eyes. 'Unless he's apologised . . . ? Come on, I need to know everything.

What's he like? Do you still *lurve* him or is he more like a brother to you now that he's living in the same house? Hey, has he painted his walls black yet? That's what Goths do, you know.'

'Stop!' cried Emily. She put down the tweezers in case she was tempted to use them as a weapon on her interrogator. And also because the one hair that she'd ripped from her brow had hurt like crazy and she needed to recover before she tried for a second one. 'If you'll stop asking questions for one minute, I'll tell you.' But what could she tell Maia? That Robert had a split personality? It felt disloyal even to think of doing that to him. Plus her best friend would think he was a total weirdo.

Maia replaced the lid on the Urban Sunset and looked expectant.

'He's not just a mountain-biking nut,' Emily said in a rush. 'He goes out at dusk and cycles in the dark. Who would do that? He wears torches on his cycling helmet that make him look like an alien and after he comes back covered in mud; he spends hours in the garage, washing down his bike that he's just muddied. And then polishes it. The next night, when any sensible person would be watching TV, he heads off across the moors on his bike again. And he brings it back, plastered with mud, again. So he cleans it. *Again*. I seriously think he's got OCD.'

Maia frowned. 'Or he just likes a clean bike.'

'Dunno.' Emily shrugged. 'Honestly, I haven't seen him much. He's either out or going through his lines with my dad. For some reason Dad's been helping him a lot. Probably because he's got the star part. Maybe he'd be doing the same for me if I was Cathy.' Emily gave a shrug and Maia looked at her sympathetically. It would take a long time for her to get over the pain of Lexie being cast as Cathy. 'Anyway,' Emily continued, 'we've walked to school once, but that's about it.'

'So do you still fancy him, or what?' said Maia.

Emily could feel her cheeks reddening. She wanted to tell Maia everything: like how much she really liked Charming Robert, and had a soft spot for Miserable Robert too, despite the fact he had been horrible to her. And how Charming Robert had said she was a handful and should have been Cathy, and that she didn't have a clue whether this was proof of his undying love or not. But she just couldn't; it sounded so stupid, even in her head.

Avoiding the question and Maia's piercing gaze, Emily looked out at sun-dappled moors framed by the old sash window . . . and before she could stifle it, an involuntary 'Oh' had escaped her.

Maia was onto her immediately. 'What's up?' she said, her head spinning round to look out of the window too. Robert was heading uphill, far faster than was surely possible on a mountain bike. 'Oh . . .' she said. 'I see.'

With a Herculean effort, Emily managed to rearrange her expression from love-struck to wistful by the time Maia looked back. 'I do like him,' she said, softly, 'but I reckon he's one of those late-starters who won't like girls until he's about eighteen.' Silently she congratulated herself. This sounded plausible even to her. And it gave her about four years until she looked a fool for not winning his affections.

Maia seemed to accept this dodgy reasoning. 'Why is it that the good-looking ones are always so slow?' she said, shaking her head sadly. 'It's criminal.' She changed tack. 'And the Granny Annexe . . . what's he done to that?'

'Haven't been inside it since he arrived,' Emily admitted.

A wicked glint appeared in Maia's eyes. 'Then why don't we go and check it out now?' she said. 'If Robert's just gone out, the coast's clear.'

At once Emily felt just a little bit sick. She swallowed. 'But it's an invasion of his privacy,' she said. 'We can't.'

We really could was the devilishly tempting thought that pinged into her head. *There's no lock on the door.*

'It's his room,' Emily added.

And it's my house.

'And what if he found us there?'

Don't be stupid. It's a sunny afternoon. He'll be gone for hours. He'll never know. Just think, I might find out all about his inner psyche, and how to make him fall for me . . .

'OK, then,' she relented, stunned at how fiendishly clever her inner thoughts were. Maybe she ought to listen to them more often.

Squaring her shoulders and doing her best to ignore her misgivings, Emily followed her intrepid friend downstairs, along the length of the gloomy hall and up the narrow flight of stairs that led to the Granny Annexe, feeling more anxious by the second. Somehow Maia managed to do a skilful shimmy on the stairs that meant Emily reached the top step first. Great. So she was doing the actual breaking and entering, when it hadn't even been her idea.

Maia nudged her from behind and Emily put a tentative hand on the door knob, twisting it gently. It swung open and she stepped inside. A woody-scented deodorant wafted by. It was remarkably pleasant and made her think at once of the moors in summertime and—

'Will you get a move on?' said Maia.

'Quit bugging me!' snapped Emily. But she crept forward anyway and pushed open the door to the tiny living room. 'Whoa . . .' she breathed. She wasn't sure what she'd been expecting, but she never thought he could be responsible for anything as mad as this: it was almost exactly the same as when Auntie O lived here.

Maia came to stand next to her, staring in disgust at the lack of chaos. 'I thought he was meant to be a Goth?' she said. 'Pathetic.'

The pile of mostly black washing that sat on the sofa was the only clue that Robert was living here. Otherwise the place was scarily neat. It was all very disappointing.

'Told you he had OCD,' Emily said to Maia. She pointed to the clean clothes that were folded so precisely their sharp edges could have delivered a nasty cut. Then she cast her eye about the room. There must be something here. She reminded herself that the boy had lived here for five days now. Yet she knew nothing about him. Like, where was the rest of his family? Where did he come from?

'Let's check out his bedroom,' said Maia.

'No!' That was taking things a step too far – and it was making Emily's stomach churn in a really uncomfortable way too. 'We can't,' she said.

But Maia was already there, which left Emily with only one course of action: follow her. But the bedroom was as orderly and uncluttered as the living room. There were no family photos and no *I heart Emily* doodles on a school book. There weren't even any pants on the floor. Emily was starting to wonder if he was actually human. Or was it just simply that he felt so out of place here that he hadn't bothered to make it look like home? Who knew.

Skrawwwwwwk!

It was the sound of harshly applied brakes. The awful scraping noise was swiftly followed by the stuttering of rubber tyres. It was a mountain bike, had to be. And it had just careered to a halt beneath the bedroom window. It took a few seconds for the truth to sink in. The worst thing possible had just happened.

Robert was back.

Emily and Maia stared at each other in terror

for a long moment. And then a gentle clip-clopping noise began to walk – no, *run* – around the edge of the house.

'It's his cycling shoes!' gasped Emily, suddenly out of breath even though she hadn't moved a muscle. 'They've got special metal bits on the soles and they clip onto his bike pedals—'

'I don't care if he cycles in stilettos!' hissed Maia. 'Run, before he finds us here!'

Tumbling down the narrow staircase as if they were being chased by wild dogs, the two girls had just staggered into the hall when the back door slammed, echoing throughout the house.

'In . . . here . . .' croaked Emily, whose voice was refusing to behave. The clip-clopping was getting closer, crossing the kitchen now . . . Hastily, she shoved Maia into the living room, and zapped the remote control at the television. It flickered into life as they flung themselves onto the brown velvet sofa.

'Er, hi,' said Robert. He was standing in the doorway, wearing a close-fitting black fleece and black shorts bedecked with so many bulging pockets that Emily figured it must take him about half an hour to find anything.

'That was a q-q-quick bike ride,' Emily managed.

'Forgot my bike pump,' said Robert, giving a wry grin that served the dual purpose of identifying him as Charming Robert and churning the contents of Emily's stomach. He peered round the door. 'Didn't see you there,' he said. 'It's Maia, isn't it?'

Maia nodded dumbly, her teeth clenched together into an unnatural smile.

'What are you two watching?'

'Erm . . .' Emily had no idea. She looked at the television, where a bunch of BMXers were skidding and bunny-hopping around a muddy track. *Oh no.* They'd been rumbled. Robert was never going to believe that they'd been watching this rubbish. Her eyes flicked towards him, but he wasn't even looking her way, instead nodding his approval as a BMX rider soared into the air, spun his handlebars – twice – and then landed neatly.

'I didn't know you were into this sort of thing,' Robert said.

'Oh, Emily loves cycling,' said Maia, still wearing the fixed grin that was beginning to make her look quite mad.

Emily elbowed her in the ribs. This was not helping.

'This is a bit more than cycling,' said Robert, apparently oblivious to any weird behaviour.

Bizarrely he looked the happiest Emily had ever seen him. 'You've got to be hardcore to attempt these tricks,' he added, wandering further into the room. Eyes still trained on the TV, he sat down on the arm of the sofa, just millimetres away from Emily.

And then, just as she was trying to decide whether she felt hot because of their break-neck escape, or if it was in fact because Robert really was very close, he leaped off the sofa as if he'd been stung.

'*Wooooaaarghhh!*' he cried.

Emily closed her eyes, feeling a curious relief. This was it. They'd been discovered. And now Robert was furious. The words *I'm so sorry* teetered on the tip of her tongue, more queuing up behind, ready to shove the whole mortifying confession into the public domain. She took a breath. 'I'm s—'

'I can't stand that stuff,' Robert said, shivering.

Emily opened her eyes and stared at him. 'Eh?'

'Velvet,' explained Robert. '*Urgh.* It totally freaks me out.'

A weird snorting noise came from the other end of the sofa. It was Maia, laughing.

Emily was about to throw a heavy object at her, when her own lips began to tremble uncontrollably and then she was laughing too. He didn't know they'd snooped. They were in the clear.

'It's *not* funny,' said Robert, but not even he could manage to keep a straight face and a moment later he joined in, accidentally touching the sofa and then leaping away from it once more, which set everyone off again.

'Soooo . . .' Robert dragged the word out as he backed out of the room, still staring at the TV. 'I'd like to join you, but I promised myself a marathon bike ride . . .' He stopped, watching as the intrepid BMXer did something so impossible that Emily felt dizzy watching it. 'Wow! Did you see that? He went off that quarter-pipe ramp, did a turn down back flip, and finished with an X-UP 180. So cool.'

'Cool,' Emily repeated. It had been cool, but so had Robert. She didn't think she'd ever seen him so animated. Not off stage anyway.

'Bye, then,' Robert said to Emily. 'See you at school on Monday, um . . . Maia.'

He was barely out of the room before Maia spoke. 'What's up with him?' she whispered. 'He spoke and smiled. Emily, he laughed.'

Until now Emily had almost felt like she was making it up. But someone else had seen both sides of Robert and the relief was amazing. 'It's like he's a different person when he's not at school,' she said. 'I wanted to tell you but it just sounded weird.'

'Yeah,' said Maia. 'He's, well . . . *nice*.'

'I know,' said Emily.

'What a shame that you're not going to be Cathy.' Maia sighed. 'You two would have been amazing together—'

'Shh!' Emily hissed. Footsteps were tapping back up the hall.

It was Robert, just as hot as before, but with much pinker cheeks. 'Hey, Emily?'

Her composure in tatters, all Emily could manage was, 'Yeah?'

'If you like cycling then we should go out for a ride sometime. Up on the moors, maybe?'

The last time Emily had ridden a bike, she'd been in single figures. Her bike – a shopper with sit-up-and-beg handlebars and a basket – was held together by rust. There was no way it would make it to the end of the drive, never mind to the moors. So there was only one answer really. 'OK,' she said.

With a brief nod, he was gone again.

Emily turned to Maia, who sprang off the sofa and began performing a solo Mexican wave. 'Emily!' she said. 'He asked you out!'

The muddy BMXer on TV did a backflip.

And so did Emily's heart.

Chapter Ten

Church bells woke Emily the next morning, chiming softly from across the moor. She peered at the alarm clock and groaned: 9:07am? No one was awake at this time on a Sunday. Except the bell-ringers. And probably Mum, who Emily remembered was on her way back from NYC on the red-eye flight. So, actually, quite a few people were awake. But not Emily. Clenching her eyes shut, she dived back under the duvet. There was no way *she* was getting up this early.

The bells kept ringing. Gentle crescendos and solemn *dongs*.

Emily pulled her pillow over her head.

The art homework she'd ignored for the last six days joined in with the bells, taunting her from inside the school bag she'd slung into the corner of the room. *Paint a watercolour that depicts an emotion*, Mr Scragg had told them. It was due in tomorrow morning, which meant that Emily had about twenty-four hours to create a masterpiece, but would probably knock something out during the X-factor results show tonight.

Downstairs the oven timer beeped one, two, three ... eight, nine ... sixteen, *seventeen times* before it was silenced. Were they deaf downstairs? Actually if Auntie O was in the kitchen, the answer was: pretty much.

Emily crawled tortoise-like from beneath the duvet and squinted at the clock: 9:09am. She sighed and admitted defeat, sliding down the bunk-bed ladder past the blissfully slumbering Jenna, who could sleep through a thunderstorm. Emily was briefly tempted to wake her sister as payback for her snoring, but then she reasoned that if Jenna – who appeared to be wearing Emily's *best pyjamas* – was asleep, then at least she wasn't being annoying. Feeling oddly virtuous, she slung on her bobbly purple dressing gown and crept downstairs. Bright sunshine poured through the kitchen windows, making everything shine like an advert for lemony bleach.

'How's my favourite Nelly Dean this morning?' sang Auntie O, looking up from her crossword.

Emily smiled. 'Where's Dad?'

'He's taken a bunch of boy scouts base jumping,' said Auntie O. She frowned. 'Or was it baseball . . . ? Anyway, he'll be back after lunch.'

Disappointment coursed through Emily. Sometimes she really wished that Dad was around a bit more. A thought occurred to her, 'Did Robert go with him . . . ?'

'Maybe,' her great-aunt replied. 'I thought of popping a cup of tea up to the lad and then I was worried about invading – what was it they called it on the radio? – Ah, yes, his personal body space. So I'm not sure if he's in or not.'

Burning with guilt, Emily helped herself to lukewarm toast and poured herself a mug of tea. She splashed in milk and watched in disgust as the tea turned an unappetising orange. '*Urgh*.' She sipped it cautiously. It was cold.

'How are the rehearsals going?' asked Auntie O. 'I've been thinking . . . If your dad's helping Robert with his lines, why don't I give you a hand with yours?'

Emily pulled a face. So far she'd just read from the script at rehearsals, unlike some people. Well, one person. Robert knew his lines so well that he didn't even have to glance at a script. He was really taking it seriously. What was his secret? 'That's really kind of you,' she said, 'but I need to get my head round them first. Then it'd be great to practise.'

Auntie O nodded and then flicked through the pages of her *Woman's Weekly*. 'Whenever you like, darling.'

Sunday loomed emptily ahead of Emily. Jenna was occupying her bedroom, so she couldn't mooch around there. There was no Maia, either. She'd gone to visit relatives for the day. Emily had half-hoped to bump into Robert, to check that he'd really meant it about the bike ride *and* to make him fully aware of her complete lack of fitness. But if he was out, then so were her chances of seeing him.

What should Emily do?

Well, the one thing she should be doing was learning her lines. Robert had shown them all how much easier it was when you didn't have to read from the script. And Auntie O's offer to help was making her feel even more guilty that she hadn't learned them yet. It was a no-brainer really. Today she'd get her head round Nelly Dean's lines. And she knew the perfect place to do it.

Ten minutes later Emily stood at the gate. Upton lay below her, its old narrow streets dipping down and out of sight, and then rising up again as they followed the contours of the valley. The autumn sun had climbed high enough to make the slate rooftops of the old northern town shine silver. It looked really beautiful today. But despite the sun, it was seriously chilly and for a moment Emily was tempted to head downhill and find a café – one that sold massive lattes.

No. Her mind was made up. She was going the other way. Up.

Emily tucked her script into an inside pocket, then zipped up her hoodie as high her nose and rubbed her chin against the fleecy lining. She jammed already cold hands in the pockets of her jeans. Really she should go back for 'something sensible' to wear. But once she did that, Emily knew that Jenna or her great aunt would waylay her and then her plan would be thwarted. Anyway once she got going, she'd be too hot if anything.

Emily squinted up at the clear, blue sky and

smiled. It was a truly glorious day, made still more dazzling by the many weeks of rain and wind that had preceded it. She pushed open the gate and strode along the road away from the house, past the ancient church and its tiny graveyard, turning up the narrow lane that led to the edge of the moor. It was a dead end, finishing in a dry-stone wall that was topped with a wooden stile. She clambered over and breathed deeply. She neatly side-stepped the chocolaty marbles left by an inconsiderate sheep and congratulated herself on choosing appropriate footwear, even if she didn't have a coat. Dad always made sure that their hiking boots were sturdy enough to withstand raging torrents and snowdrifts, so sheep poo was no problem.

She set off up the hill, swinging her arms in circles as she'd once been told to do on a school ski trip. It was some sort of centrifugal nonsense that was supposed to make all the blood rush to her fingertips and magically warm her up. Firmly pushing thoughts of her cosy jacket to the back of her mind, she marched on, heather swishing round her ankles.

Vowing not to look back until she reached the top, Emily went up ... up ... *oof* ... up ...

until, with a ragged sigh of relief, she turned and stared. She'd come so far that Upton had sunk out of sight. All around was moorland, stretching away in every direction, the strong breeze rippling the heather, transforming it into a vast sea of undulating loveliness.

'Wow.'

No matter how many times Emily came up here – and goodness knows Dad had made them do it enough – she never grew tired of its wild beauty. This was way better than homework. She thought about Other Emily. The one who'd written *Wuthering Heights*. Emily *Brontë*. She must have experienced this too. The thought made her feel suddenly in touch with the long-dead author and the words of the play ran through her mind.

A dark shadow raced across the moor and swiftly engulfed her. Emily looked up to see that the sun was now hidden behind a lone cloud. Suddenly it was freezing and Emily was regretting just wearing her hoodie. The cloud scudded away almost at once and she felt the faint warmth of the sun on her face. But as she shaded her eyes and stared into the wind, she saw that the solitary cloud was just an outrider. In the west a bank of menacing rainclouds loomed, moving steadily towards her.

Emily pulled up her hood and yanked the cord tight, so that just her eyes and nose were visible. How long had she been walking? It could have been minutes or hours – she didn't have a clue. A swift glance at her bare wrist revealed that she wasn't going to get any hints there. *Idiot*. She remembered seeing her watch that morning, sitting on the chest-of-drawers. *Beside her mobile phone*. So she couldn't tell anyone where she was either.

The sun vanished again and Emily saw that she had less time than she'd thought. The leaden clouds were nearer now. Darker too. She heard the faint rumble of thunder.

Oh, perfect.

Emily had to make a choice – and preferably before she was drenched. Should she head home or keep going? She looked back the way she'd come. Home was out of sight. Besides there was no way she'd get back before the storm.

Just past a copse of dead trees a few hundred metres away, there was an outcrop of rocks that overlooked the next valley. Before Divorce, Emily, Jenna, Mum and Dad had once picnicked beneath the overhang. It was a lovely spot – sheltered and secluded. This was where she'd planned to learn her lines, but it would also be the perfect place for sitting out a storm.

Decision made, she sprinted forward. She stumbled through the heather, her hood pulled low to block out the bitter wind that had sprung up, and she kept her eyes down so she didn't trip over anything. Slowing to check that she was still heading the right way, Emily saw the familiar rocks outlined against the battleship-grey sky. Not far now.

She jogged the last few steps and staggered to a halt on top of the outcrop. And then, coming from somewhere beneath her feet, she heard a deep voice. It trembled with anger.

'. . . *I have a mind to speak a few words now, while we are at it – I want you to be aware that I know you have treated me infernally – infernally! Do you hear? And if you flatter yourself that I don't perceive it, you are a fool – and if you think I can be consoled by sweet words you are an idiot – and if you fancy I'll suffer . . . that I'll suffer . . .* Oh, God. What comes next? *And if you fancy that I'll suffer unrevenged—*'

'Heathcliff . . . ?' Emily breathed.

Despite the wind and rain, he heard her. 'Hello?'

Emily froze. This was officially the middle of

nowhere. Yet *he* was here. Robert had copied her brilliant idea – and done it first. She shook her head, it couldn't be *him*, could it? He'd gone out with Dad. Auntie O had told her so. Then Emily remembered that actually, she hadn't.

He was right here, right now.

Chapter Eleven

'Who's there?' called Robert, interrupting Emily's silent victory dance. 'You'd better come and shelter, or you're going to get *really* wet in a minute.'

As if this was the signal the dark clouds had been waiting for, the first fat raindrops began to splat down on Emily. A curious shyness made her hold back. She didn't want Robert to think that she was one of those weird stalker types. But the rain was quickly soaking into the cotton of her hoodie so, sheepishly, she made her way round the outcrop and down the steep grassy slope that ran downhill alongside it. Nestled beneath a rocky ledge, there was the picnic spot, and there was Robert McBride.

'You!' He looked gobsmacked. 'What are *you* doing here?'

Emily bit her lip. 'Walking,' she said, stepping underneath the ledge and out of the rain. It had quickly increased in intensity and was now hammering down so hard that the moors were hidden from view. 'I wanted to find somewhere quiet to learn my lines,' she said, patting the A4-sized bulge inside her top.

Was it her imagination or did Robert flinch?

'Oh,' he said quickly. 'Right.' His dark eyes checked out her sodden clothes. 'It's not summer, you know.'

She shrugged. 'I'm officially an idiot. I suppose your gear is waterproof to a depth of 300 metres?'

'At least,' Robert said. He pressed his lips into a smile.

Emily shifted her weight from one foot to the other, wondering why this felt so awkward. She decided to flip Robert's question back to him. 'What are you doing here?' she asked.

Instead of answering he pointed to his mountain bike, which was lying on its side like a wounded animal.

Emily stared at the bike. Two wheels, handlebars, frame and— *Ouch*! The saddle looked about as comfortable as a razor blade. But otherwise it looked fine. 'What's wrong with it?' she said.

Lips that yesterday had been soft, luscious and totally kissable were now yanked into a sneer. 'I thought you knew about bikes. How do you think it's going to work without one of these?' Robert raised oily hands and she saw that there was a long chain dangling from them, like a dirty, outsize necklace.

A *broken* necklace.

'Oh,' she said, feeling stupid. This really was *not* going well.

'I bust a link in my chain and this seemed as good a place as any to fix it,' he said, crouching down beside his bike. He was silent for a few seconds and then turned to her. 'Want to give me a hand?'

Emily nodded, relief flooding through her as Robert carefully wound the chain into place. He was back to normal again. Good. Miserable Robert's guest appearance had reminded her just how much she liked his cheerier counterpart. Charming Robert handed her the two ends of the chain and then rummaged in his backpack. He used the small tool he found inside to fasten the ends together again.

'Sorted.' He was so close that she could see the way his mouth bunched more on one side than the other when he smiled. 'Cheers,' he added.

For a few seconds they stared at each other. Then the cave turned an intense, dazzling white, before plunging into darkness. A thunderclap boomed, so loud that it seemed to make the air tremble. Emily shot to her feet. She wasn't scared, but her vision was filled with bright dancing spots and her ears were singing. There must be *squillions* of megawatts of electricity buzzing around. She could almost *feel* them and felt suddenly jittery. The lightning couldn't get to them in here, could it?

She said the first thing that came into her head and should have stayed in her head, if the look on Robert's face was anything to go by. 'Were you practising your lines when I arrived?'

He stiffened with anger. 'So what if I was?'

Emily could have slapped herself. Somehow she'd made him angry again. But if she stopped talking now it wasn't going to make things any better. He was already mad. And anyway there was something that just didn't stack up. 'Where's your script, then?' she asked. She couldn't see it anywhere.

Robert tapped his head with one finger. 'In here.'

'All of it?'

'Almost.'

'Wow.' Emily's admiration soared as she realised just how brilliant he must be to know the whole play by heart. She loved acting, but even after countless am-dram performances, she'd never found a shortcut for learning lines. 'What's your secret? Have you got a photographic memory or something?'

'Oh give it a rest, will you?' He spat the words out, sounding as if he were struggling to keep his temper. 'I don't need *you* making fun of me too.'

'You what?' Emily was stunned. If Robert acted like this on stage, the audience would be hooked. But she wasn't watching his dark, angry eyes and heavy brow from the safety of the back row. It was just the two of them in the middle of an empty moor, in a cave. Emily was close enough to see his Adam's apple bobbing up and down as he swallowed. Behind him the rain formed an impenetrable curtain, blocking everything outside the cave from view.

Under normal circumstances, this would be *so* romantic ... Stormy weather? *Check*. Gorgeous boy? *Check*. All alone? *Check*. But by now, Robert should definitely be tracing a finger down the side of her face and telling her how beautiful she was, just before diving in for a long, slow kiss.

The problem was, he actually looked like he wanted to punch her.

Emily kissed the kiss goodbye.

But just as the tension in the cave peaked, Robert broke eye contact and turned his back. He began ramming tools into his hi-tech backpack.

Great. Now he was ignoring her. Released from his angry glare, Emily slid down the wall, her hoodie snagging on the rough rock face. She reached the ground with a thump and stayed there, elbows balanced on the damp denim clinging to her knees. The silences after each thunderclap were growing longer as the storm moved further away. But still the rain fell.

Time yawned.

Emily decided to have one last try before her bottom went totally numb. If he didn't open up to her this time, she'd give up. 'I wasn't making fun of you,' she said softly to Robert's back. 'I don't know what I've done to upset you, but I do think you're amazing.'

Robert turned to stare.

'On stage.' Emily blushed. 'You're a great actor, I mean.' He still hadn't spoken, so she added, 'So, would you like to read through a couple of scenes with me? I'd love to know how you do it—'

'Stop it!' Robert shouted, angrier now than she'd ever seen him. 'You're always doing it. Always staring at me as if you're trying to catch me out. It's not easy living in someone else's house, you know. It's not easy when— Oh, forget it.' He actually looked as if he was going to cry. And then his expression darkened and he was just plain furious once more. 'You try fitting in when everyone's watching you and willing you to fail.'

'What?' If Emily's back hadn't been pressed firmly to the wall, she would have looked over her shoulder to see if there was someone else there who deserved the terrible things he was saying. She couldn't believe he was talking to *her*. Slack-jawed, she stared up at him. 'B-but yesterday was cool,' she croaked. 'Wasn't it?'

He gave a short laugh. 'As if you really like BMXing. Bet you can't wait to tell everyone that, like you couldn't wait to tell them about me moving into yours. *Cheers*.'

This was so unfair that Emily was starting to get mad too. 'Do you know what you are, Robert

120

McBride?' she said. 'You're as miserable and as mean as your stupid character.'

'And you're as dull as yours,' he flung back at her. 'At least Heathcliff *does* stuff. What does Nelly Dean do? She just watches other people, sticks her nose in and gossips. At least Cathy's got a bit of life in her. Instead of asking me for acting tips, why don't you ask Lexie? She's twice the actor you'll ever be.' Pale with anger, he went to the other side of the cave and leaned one shoulder against the wall, glaring out at the storm.

Tears began to prickle at the corners of Emily's eyes. Outside the rain was as heavy as ever, but the storm itself was definitely receding now. Forget the rain. Emily was *so* out of here.

Pulling the cord on her hood tight, she struggled to her feet and, without looking back, walked from the dry cave through the dripping veil of rain and into the wildness outside. She was soaked instantly, but she didn't care. Anything was better than being insulted by someone she'd liked and had been foolish enough to think actually liked her. Scrambling up the grassy slope, she made it back to the open moor. The wind blew grey sheets of rain across the sodden ground. Wow. It was desperate up here.

As soon as Emily began to run, a sob broke from her throat and the tears that had been threatening ever since she'd heard Robert's cruel words started to fall. She swiped at her cheeks, but it made no difference. Rain and tears mingled as, choked with anguish, she tore across the moor.

After a few minutes, she heard a faint shout behind her.

She didn't look back.

Chapter Twelve

On Monday morning the A+ that Emily got in Art for the swirling vortex of red, purple and black – 'Anger' – lifted her spirits. But her black mood returned as soon as she remembered the *Wuthering Heights* rehearsal that evening. Two hours on stage with *him*.

She saw him as soon as she walked into the school hall, slumped against the ropes and talking animatedly into his mobile. He looked really miserable.

'No change there, then,' Emily muttered to herself.

'You what?' said Jason.

'Er . . . just getting into character,' Emily mumbled. But inside she was squirming with embarrassment. *Oh dear*. Now she was talking to herself.

'Cool,' said Jason, backing away slowly.

Emily let out a heavy sigh. It was all Robert's fault.

Whack!

The double doors swung open to reveal Miss Edwards. 'Hello!' she cried, with far too much enthusiasm for a Monday. 'I'm sure you've all finished reading the novel version of *Wuthering Heights* by now.' She looked around them, all puppy-dog eager. 'Yes . . . ?'

No one spoke.

Emily examined her fingernails. She had meant to get round to it, but somehow hadn't. She decided to blame Robert for that too. He was the one messing with her head.

'Well, never mind,' Miss Edwards said softly. Then, in the next breath, her oomph was back. 'Anyway we're going to do a complete read-through of the script today. Don't worry too much about the stage directions – I'd just like you all to get to grips with the storyline. Then you can begin to empathise with the characters and their motivation. It's easier to act in a play when you know exactly what's going on. And maybe you could all think about reading the book afterwards . . . ?'

Emily nodded uncertainly.

It all sounded a bit dull.

Like Nelly Dean. Like you.

The words echoed nastily, but Emily did her best to ignore them and Robert McBride, who was lurking at the blurry edges of her vision. She turned her attention instead to Miss Edwards, who was busy arranging chairs into a cosy circle.

'What's this? Some sort of self-help group?' sneered Lexie. 'Actors Anonymous?'

Obligingly Daniel roared with laughter.

Ruby rolled her eyes. 'He's trying to stay in her good books,' she said under her breath. 'I bet she's going to finish with him.'

'Eh?' said Emily. 'How do you work that one out?'

'She's done it before,' said Ruby. 'Lexie pushes boys away when she's had enough of them. I give it a week.'

'Rubbish,' said Emily. But her eyes followed Lexie as she chose a seat in the circle and then beckoned one of her fans to sit beside her. When Daniel made for the spare seat on her other side, Lexie smiled sweetly and told him that Cathy and

Heathcliff really needed to sit together. Wearing a hurt expression, he moved away.

'Robert!' called Lexie. 'Here!'

He looked surprised, but Robert didn't argue and Emily breathed in sharply. Right. Well that suited her just fine. Lexie was welcome to him. She and Robert were as rude as each other.

After a few false starts and fluffed lines, which were almost drowned out by the nervous rustling of paper and clearing of throats, they got going. Whenever there was a particularly tricky scene, Miss Edwards cut in with a handy explanation of what was going on. Emily had to admit that it was all starting to make sense. Like many of them, she'd read just a few chapters of the original and then abandoned the book in favour of the slimmed-down script, but she vowed to give *Wuthering Heights* another go, starting tonight.

During one of the frequent – and very long – sections of the play during which Nelly Dean had precisely zero to say, Emily watched the faces of the other students. As they gradually forgot that they were being watched, the actors started to put real feeling into their words. And as Robert spoke, all eyes were drawn to him. He stormed and sulked so magnificently that Emily almost forgot what an idiot he was. Almost.

'Good,' Miss Edwards announced at the end. '*Really* good.' She smiled at them all. 'Now, I have a surprise for you.'

'Oh, goody,' said Lexie.

The Drama teacher ignored her. 'I thought that you'd all benefit enormously from a trip to Emily Brontë's own home. So I've organised a trip to Haworth. Once you see where she wrote and find out a little more about this star of English literature, then I'm sure you'll start to appreciate what an achievement it was for her to write such a wonderfully imaginative and totally original book.'

'Er . . . when is this?' asked Emily. It had better not be this Saturday because that was when she and Maia were going shopping. And not just any old shopping either, it was all planned. First they were hitting the mid-season sales. Then they were stopping for coffee and muffins. And then they were hitting the sales again. Followed by all-they-could-eat pizza and as-much-as-they-could-drink Coke. And in the afternoon they were going to trawl through every single charity shop in town, in search of the one-off bargains that magazines were always bleating on about. And then they were going to squeeze in some of those delicious goo-filled doughnuts before going home. They weren't seeing so much of each other now the rehearsals were gathering pace. This Saturday would be just like old times.

'It's this Saturday,' said Miss Edwards proudly. She shook back her glossy red-brown hair and beamed at the circle of underwhelmed students as if expecting a round of applause.

'But that's . . . the weekend,' said Daniel slowly.

Miss Edwards' smile slipped just a little. 'Yes, that's true,' she said, blithely ignoring the groans that rippled around the circle. 'But we can't go on a school day, can we? What about lessons?'

Emily sighed. She was going to be in so much trouble with Maia.

'I'll be inviting all of the backstage team to join us,' said Miss Edwards. 'I'm sure they'd love to come too.'

Phew. That meant Maia would be coming. Emily wondered what the shops were like in Haworth, because the museum wasn't going to take long.

'Until Thursday, then,' said the drama teacher, wrapping it up.

The actors stretched and yawned. Gathering up

her script, Emily shrugged on her waterproof coat and headed for the door, cannoning into a figure in a grey duffel coat.

'Er . . .' he said. 'I, er . . .'

Emily scowled at Robert. This was the first time he'd spoken to her since his outburst on Sunday. If 'er' was all he could manage, then she wasn't interested. 'Yeah, whatever,' she said, brushing him aside and storming out of the hall. She wasn't just going to put up with his behaviour. She would stand up and be a handful like Catherine Earnshaw. Whatever he may think, she was no Nelly Dean.

For once it wasn't raining, and Emily powered up the hill and was home in record time. She crashed through the back door and frowned at the person sitting at the kitchen table. It was Dad. *Oh*. He wouldn't understand.

Emily smiled at him. 'Sorry, wrong relative.' Ignoring his confused expression, she rushed out of the kitchen and paused for a moment in the hall, listening for clues. Aha. The television was on in the living room. She peered round the door.

'So how did you get on at the rehearsal, dear?' asked her great-aunt, her knitting needles continuing to click away at something bright yellow.

Emily stared at it and prayed that it wasn't her Christmas present.

'Have a mint.' Auntie O gestured towards a tin of beige discs.

Emily shook her head and then grimaced. 'Can you believe it? Miss Edwards is only making us go to Haworth on Saturday. It's not *fair*. I was meant to be going shopping with Maia.'

'Oh, you can always go shopping,' said Auntie O briskly. 'A trip to Haworth will be infinitely better for you. So much fun . . .' She gently put down her knitting and reached for the old paperback on the coffee table, stroking its cover gently.

It was *Wuthering Heights*.

Emily nearly screamed. Haworth . . . the Brontës . . . and always, *Heathcliff*. Was there no getting away from the stupid book? 'I give up!' she said. 'I'll be in my room.' She stomped dramatically up the wooden stairs until Dad hollered at her that it sounded as if she was felling a tree and could she please keep the noise down.

Emily flung open her bedroom door. But Jenna was already there. She glared at Emily accusingly from the middle of a floor that was carpeted with school books.

'I'm doing my homework,' Jenna said, primly

flicking through a magazine. 'You'd better not disturb me with any of that play nonsense.'

So angry she couldn't speak, Emily clambered up to the top bunk and sulked for a few minutes about how everyone around here was determined to make her live and breathe *Wuthering Heights*, when she was sick of the very sight of it.

They were *all* at it: Auntie O loved the book; Miss Edwards was nigh on evangelical about the play. And then there was Robert . . . The one who was nice one minute and nasty the next. The one with the voice that made her think of harsh winds and moors and softly purple heather and summer days and cold, cold nights . . .

Angrily she snatched *Wuthering Heights* out of her bag.

She might as well see what all the fuss was about.

Chapter Thirteen

'Is there a New Look?' Maia grumbled as the coach growled round a corner and reached the foot of a steep hill. She stared out of the slightly grimy window. 'Bet there isn't.'

'Where's the amusement arcade?' roared a boy from the back seats. 'Mum told me there was a really big one.'

'It's next to the funfair and the tattoo parlour,' said Maia drily.

Emily stifled a giggle. At least she wasn't that gullible. She leaned back and wondered if she'd look like a total geek if she pulled *Wuthering Heights* out of her bag and read a couple of pages.

She was starting to get into it, even the writing, which was old-fashioned, but sort of cool. Cathy was fierce and headstrong, and a thoroughly terrifying ghost. Emily had hardly been able to sleep after reading the first few chapters. Heathcliff was savage, strong-willed and angry. And even though Emily still couldn't work out whether she actually *liked* either of the main characters, their love-hate relationship and the passion between them had her gripped. Not that she was going to admit that to anyone, of course. Reluctantly she decided against reading it. Maia would kill herself laughing. Anyway they were almost there.

The old coach coughed asthmatically as it turned into the car park and then finally stopped. Its door opened with a sigh.

Miss Edwards sprang to her feet and blocked the exit. 'Don't move,' she warned.

'Cool idea,' said Sam. But the force of Miss Edwards' stare flung him back in his seat. 'Joking,' he muttered.

Obviously aware that she had everyone's attention for a limited time, the drama teacher launched into her briefing. They would all – and that meant *everyone* – visit the Brontë Parsonage Museum first. They'd all behave. They'd all remember that they were representing their school. There would be no running, shouting or pushing . . . Emily was usually able to keep her rebellious streak in check, but the instructional overload was making her feel like doing something really dumb, like bouncing on Emily Brontë's antique bed. She buttoned up her grey duffel coat and – while Miss Edwards banged on and on – reached into her bag. Her fingertips touched the smooth bendiness of the paperback hidden there. She blushed.

'. . . and remember to be polite,' finished Miss Edwards. The words were barely out of her mouth before the frontrunners shouldered her aside and began clambering off the coach.

'Come on,' said Maia. 'Let's get the museum over and done with.'

'OK.' Emily grinned and then she shimmied along the narrow aisle after the others. She kept her head down so that Miss Edwards didn't make eye contact and force her to discuss something terminally dull like cholera in the nineteenth century. But although staring at the floor was an excellent way to dodge the teacher, it wasn't to be recommended as an object-avoidance tactic. If Emily had been looking where she was going, she would have spotted the tall, wide-shouldered, black-clad thing just outside the coach instead of cannoning right into it.

'Ooof!' it groaned.

He groaned.

Emily groaned too. It seemed rude not to.

'Um . . . hi,' she said to Robert. Of course it was *him*. It wasn't like she bumped into anyone else these days. Was he magnetic or something?

'Hi,' he replied.

OK. What came next? For Emily to say 'hi' again would be lame. *Beyond* lame. It was nearly a week since he'd yelled at her on the moor. She'd ignored him and had calmed down a bit now. She didn't hate him *quite* as much; it was more like a mild loathing. She had to say something – anything would do.

There was an uncomfortable silence, during which Emily wondered if she'd accidentally spoken aloud. But her mouth felt so dry and rusty that she realised she couldn't have said a word without a good glug of engine oil. She swallowed with difficulty. Then, shifting from one foot to the other, she risked a glance at Robert, who was staring down at her in this really intense way that was making her insides flip.

135

'Look . . .' he started.

'I . . .' she croaked. 'I . . . I . . .' Oh no. Now she sounded like a car starting. And she didn't even know how the rest of the sentence went yet. Privately she was hoping that it would burst from her lips, fully formed and eloquent. Something the Brontës would be proud of. 'I—'

'Oy!'

Maia was standing at the bottom of the high street, hands on hips. 'Aren't you pair finished yet?' she shouted. 'Only we've got to look round a boring museum before we have clearance to eat, so I'd like to get started before my stomach collapses in on itself like a black hole.'

Emily shouldered her bag and marched the few steps that lay between her and her so-called best friend. 'You are so embarrassing and so wrong!' she hissed, once she reached her. 'I told you last week that I wouldn't like him if he were the last boy in Yorkshire. Let's go.'

'I get it,' said Maia. 'You hate him, right?'

'Yes.' Emily marched up the street, trying to keep her balance on the cobbles. 'I do.'

But even as she said it Emily knew this wasn't the truth. Not even close.

*

The Brontë Parsonage Museum was at the top of a very steep hill, nestled among sombre grey houses. The parsonage itself was a wide, squat building with five tall, leaded windows above, four below and a grand front door in the middle. It looked serious and sedate. A steady stream of visitors flowed through the door and disappeared inside.

Emily decided that the place had an aura of melancholy. She wasn't sure if she wanted to go in.

'Posh, isn't it?' said Maia, looking puzzled. 'I was expecting more of a ruin, like the gloomy, miserable old *Wuthering Heights* that we're painting on the backdrop. If I ever *see* a tin of black paint again, I'm going to lose the plot.'

'They had such unbelievable imaginations, it didn't matter *where* they lived ...' said Miss Edwards, who was standing nearby.

'Talking to herself,' Lexie told her entourage. She twirled a finger around in the air. 'Totally cuckoo.'

The drama teacher was too busy gazing awestruck at the parsonage to notice.

'So Mr Brontë was the vicar,' said Maia. She looked over to the church that was barely a stone's throw away from the old parsonage. 'Not much of a commute, was it?'

Emily spluttered.

'The house came with the job.' The teacher smiled serenely. Apparently nothing was going to upset her today. 'Emily Brontë's father was the perpetual curate.'

'Oh,' said Maia. She turned to Emily and mouthed, '*What?*'

Emily shrugged, trying not to laugh again. She hadn't a clue either.

'Everyone here?' called Miss Edwards.

'Oh no . . .' muttered Sam. 'Not another speech.'

But it was just a headcount. Briskly the teacher ushered them inside.

Emily was one of the last to go in. But not *the* last, because she knew that Robert hadn't gone before her, which meant that he must be behind her somewhere. The thought made her feel nervous. But she told herself that was stupid. It wasn't as if he'd look at her in that intense way again – though she wished he *would* because, actually, she couldn't stop thinking about it.

As Emily went into the crowded hall with the others, a curious reverence seemed to descend on them all. Emily forgot about Robert. Everyone spoke in hushed tones, shuffling along the narrow hall and into the tiny front room, where they peered over the rope at the perfectly preserved furniture beyond.

In and out of the tiny rooms they went, and up the narrow wooden staircase that led to the bedrooms above. They oohed and aahed over the actual dress that Charlotte Brontë had worn. It was *tiny*. And her bed was barely big enough for a child.

'They were really *short*, weren't they?' said Daniel.

'Well done, Dan,' sneered Lexie. 'Remind me to nominate you for the Sherlock Holmes Award.'

Daniel looked hurt.

'Uh-oh,' muttered Ruby, who was standing nearby. 'Told you. He's going to get the elbow *really* soon. Wonder who she's got lined up next?'

'I bet it's Robert,' Maia said under her breath.

Emily felt as if she'd been punched. Maia hadn't even been at Monday's rehearsal. 'Why would you think that?' she asked.

'She can never stand it when someone doesn't fancy her, which makes him the ultimate catch.' She caught Emily's stunned expression. 'What's up with *you*?' she hissed. 'You told me about ten minutes ago that you wouldn't go near him if he were the last boy in Yorkshire, and now you're looking all jealous because someone else is after him. Make your mind up.'

Emily sniffed haughtily and didn't reply. Truthfully she didn't know why she was shocked, because all she and Robert ever did was argue. Lexie was welcome to him.

'Yes, Daniel,' said Miss Edwards, taking pity on the publicly humiliated boy. 'In this area the average height of a man in the mid-nineteenth century was only 1.66 metres. Today it's nearer 1.78 metres. How about that?'

No one spoke. Some things were just too dull even to acknowledge.

'Anyway!' the drama teacher continued brightly. 'Follow me through to the history section of the museum. It's really *very* informative.'

'Hope it's better than your fun facts,' Maia grumbled.

It was better.

But it was shocking. Emily had never read anything so sad. *Ever*.

Reverently everyone worked their way around the display, reading about how polluted water and terrible diseases had queued up and struck down the poor Brontës one by one. First the mother, and then the children – Maria, Elizabeth, Branwell, Emily, Anne and finally Charlotte – died, until Mr Brontë was the only one left. Oh, and the Reverend Nicholls, Charlotte's widower, who went on to outlive them all.

At Branwell's death, Emily was snivelling. By Anne's, tears were trickling unchecked down her cheeks. And by the time she got to Charlotte – who lived the longest of all the Brontë children, reaching the grand old age of thirty-eight – Emily was crying like a baby. As she stared at the display cases with their mournful contents, swiping alternate cuffs across her face, she felt an arm around her shoulders.

'Oh, Maia . . .' Emily wailed. 'It's just so *tragic*.' Her eyes tightly shut in an effort to stem the flow of tears, she turned to lay her head on her friend's shoulder and was surprised when it wasn't there. Instead her face met a vertical wall of woollen coat, scratchy and warm. That was odd. Maia had been wearing a mac last time Emily had looked. She brought one hand up to hug Maia. Ah, there was her shoulder. It was higher than usual and further to the right. Strange . . . Was her best friend standing on a step? Because she hadn't remembered her wearing heels today. And *that* wasn't her usual perfume – the zingy lemon that she loved. It was muskier, sort of woody. More like . . .

Emily froze. She kept her face pressed against the woollen fabric, now damp with her tears, and her eyes tight shut. If she opened them, she knew what she was going to see and she wasn't quite ready for that. So she kept them closed for just a few seconds longer, enjoying the oddly comfortable sensation of standing in the middle of Robert McBride's hug.

'Come on,' he mumbled to her. 'Let's go.'

Reluctantly she opened her eyes and – *wow*, his face was close – examined his dark eyes for any sign of imminent rage or another wild emotion that would guarantee they'd be arguing again within seconds. No, there was none. If anything he looked as stunned as she felt.

'OK,' she said.

Ignoring all the stares and whispers, they left. And with a silent melting happiness, Emily nestled into the crook of Robert's arm. She suddenly felt as if she'd had central heating installed inside her.

Feeling as if she must be dreaming, Emily slowly descended a staircase so narrow that she and Robert had to huddle really close to fit down. She winced as she felt rather than heard his knuckles graze the wall, but there was no way she was going to offer to go ahead. Not when he was breathing softly in her ear and turning her central heating up a notch. Things like this just didn't happen to her every day – any day, actually – and Emily was going to enjoy it as long as possible.

As long as possible turned out to be about forty-five seconds.

The moment they reached the museum gift shop, Robert's hand slid from Emily's shoulder and he immediately put it out of reach by stuffing it into the pocket of his coat. She did the same. When she looked up, Robert was over by the exit, studying a rack of postcards.

'So . . .' he said. 'Feeling better?'

'Yeah,' Emily replied. 'Much. Thanks.' She heard footsteps clattering down the stairs. The others were coming. She didn't have much time. But her brain suddenly seemed filled with candyfloss and all she knew was that she really wanted him to hug her again, because . . . well, it had felt *amazing*.

How was she going to say *that*?

'OK,' Robert said, addressing the floor. 'Um . . . see you.'

'There you are!'

Emily swung round.

Maia was dancing through the shop as if she were leading an invisible conga. 'Where is he?' she demanded.

Emily looked back. He was gone, of course. 'Dunno,' she said, and her heart actually sank. She felt it.

'Did he kiss you?'

'No!' Emily tried to sound outraged, but giggled instead. She blamed the candyfloss. 'He absolutely did not.'

'Sure?' asked Maia. 'He had his arm round you. We all saw.'

Emily smiled. 'I know. But he definitely didn't kiss me.'

'Come on,' said Maia, linking her arm through Emily's. 'Let's get out of here before everyone else arrives. Then you can tell me *all* about it. Every single slushy detail.'

It was as she floated arm-in-arm with Maia down the high street that Emily's epiphany blasted all other thoughts from her head. If she thought she hated the stroppy, miserable, deep-voiced, tall and fiendishly good-looking boy, who'd done nothing but cause turmoil since he'd arrived, then she was kidding herself.

And if Lexie thought she was going to snatch him from under Emily's nose, she could think again.

The rest of the day passed in a stream of non-stop vanilla lattes as Emily analysed all the details of that hug with Maia. Emily didn't see Robert again until they all met back at the coach park and then there he was, head down, collar turned up against the wind. Gorgeous.

As eyes turned towards Emily, there was suddenly a crescendo of wolf whistles. It seemed that just about everyone had seen Robert hugging her. And it didn't matter how many times she told them that *nothing* was going on. They still whistled and sang and made Emily blush bright red. Robert stayed well out of it, burying his head in a book as soon as he got on the coach. But the jibes must have affected his concentration, because Emily noticed that he didn't turn over a single page the whole journey.

The only person who wasn't thrilled about the hug was Lexie. 'Of course he doesn't fancy Nelly—oops, *Emily*,' she told Daniel in a narked voice. 'She's *so* not his type.'

Emily ignored her.

Chapter Fourteen

On Saturday evening Jenna was safely out of the way at a sleepover, which meant that Emily had her bedroom to herself and her music LOUD. She smiled and thought about Robert. She was *still* glowing.

Dad was out too, supervising a night hike on the moors or something equally tortuous. Auntie O was in her bedroom, watching a DVD of the 1939 version of *Wuthering Heights* that she'd borrowed from the library. Emily checked on her after tea and told her all about the trip. Apart from the bit about Robert.

In return Emily's great-aunt told her that the

film starred Sir Lawrence Olivier – who was dead famous as well as being dead – as Heathcliff. Emily watched a few minutes of the grainy black-and-white picture and decided that Auntie O's Heathcliff might be admirably grumpy, but next to hers he was an amateur.

Robert was out. Emily had seen him go, watching from her hiding place behind the curtains as he wheeled his mountain bike round to the back of the house at dusk and then pedalled furiously towards the moors, his head torches glowing like cats' eyes on the motorway. Only when he was out of sight had she turned up her music – Auntie O's television next door was *very* loud – and retreated to the solitude of the top bunk to do some serious thinking.

Over and over she replayed the magical event in the museum, until she'd been through it so many times that she was starting to worry she'd wear out the memory. Or that she might be unwittingly tweaking the original to make it better . . . But as tempting as it was to ramp up the romance with a long, slow kiss, she needed to remember it *exactly* as it had happened.

Just one last time then.

She lay back against her pillow, letting her lids drop. She felt the virtual trickle of tears down her cheeks as she looked at the grim and grimmer facts about the Brontës' short lives in the museum. Yes, she was feeling the sorrow now. She was back there, tears threatening. She hurried on to the part where her lids had romantically fluttered shut and she'd dabbed at them with a lace-edged handkerchief ... *Er, no* ... She tried again, returning to the part where she'd shut her eyes and his arm had encircled her shoulders and it had been so reassuringly heavy and comforting that ...

A faint noise penetrated her daydream. She opened her eyes and propped herself up on her elbows. She'd heard something outside. No ... She must be mistaken. When she listened again, there was nothing.

Snuggling in bed once more, Emily got back to business. This was the good bit. She remembered turning to face the warmth of his coat and was sure that she'd felt the quickening heartbeat beneath the thick wool— She froze. Now she'd definitely heard something going on outside. It was a sort of clattery-banging. And there was shouting too.

'Cathy!'

What? Was there some sort of literary time warp going on here?

'Catheeeeeee!'

There was a little part of Emily that couldn't help feeling a bit freaked, as a terrifying image of the ghost of Catherine Earnshaw crept into her mind. It was probably someone playing a joke, she decided. Maybe Jenna had come back early.

Emily clambered over the edge of the bunk and did a practised slide down the wooden ladder. She padded across the room towards the window. That was where the noise was coming from. But she drew back at the last minute. What if it wasn't a practical joker but a burglar? Only Emily and Auntie O were in the house. They'd stand no chance against a masked intruder with a sawn-off shotgun. Perhaps she should ring the police first.

'Emileeeeee!'

She cocked her head on one side. The whistling of the wind had distorted the shouting . . . Whoever was outside was shouting *her* name, not Cathy's.

Crash.

That did it. Emily yanked back the curtains and stared out into the night. There was nothing there. She peered downwards, wondering if she'd actually heard the yowling of a stray cat . . . and then her legs nearly gave way beneath her, because instead she saw furious dark eyes glaring back at her through the glass.

Oh. My. God.

Emily tried to scream or shout, but her throat had tightened and all she could manage was a strangled whisper. '*Help* . . .' she mouthed pointlessly, trying to move backwards and out of danger. But her feet were stuck firm with shock. She had no choice but to gaze, frozen with fear, at the figure with the shadowy eyes and the dark, messy hair and the very dirty face. He was mouthing something back at her. She frowned. Had he lost his voice too?

Then she realised that the window was shut. *That* was why she couldn't hear him. But if she opened the window, then the mugger-murderer-type could climb in and bash her over the head with a heavy object.

She was startled out of her reverie by the sight of the intruder climbing higher and realised that he must be clinging on to the drainpipe. Well, anyone could have told him that wasn't a good idea. It was rusted right through in two places and had recently shot up to number five in Dad's never-ending to-do list, which meant that it was hazardous.

'*Get down*,' she mouthed. '*You'll fall.*'

'*Let me in*,' he mouthed back. '*Open. The. Window.*'

She stared. 'Robert?' she asked, her vocal cords magically coming back to life as her fear evaporated. She moved forward to have a closer look. It wasn't a murderer. It was *him*. 'What are you doing out there?' she said.

Robert rolled his eyes.

'Oh, sorry,' she said, pulling back the metal arm that fastened the top window and shoving it outwards so that she could hear him. She watched in horror as the window caught Robert on the chin and knocked him backwards. He flailed in midair for a couple of seconds and then lurched back towards the window, his fingers scrabbling for a handhold – and then hanging on as he found one. His fingers gripped white over the edge of the wooden frame. *Oops*. She hadn't meant for that to happen.

'What are you doing?' asked Emily, once she was sure Robert had a secure hold on the window frame and wasn't going to plummet to his death. He was so close that Emily could see that the few patches of skin that weren't splattered with mud were white with fright. She gulped. It was the first time she hadn't seen him looking cool. He really *was* scared.

'I forgot my key,' Robert gasped. 'And I knocked for *ages*, but no one heard me. So I saw the lights on in your room and decided I'd climb up before I froze to death.'

Emily edged guiltily towards her iPod and turned the music down. It wasn't surprising that neither of them had heard Robert knocking.

'*Wooarrrghhh*!' he cried. There was a horrible wrenching sound as the drainpipe came away from the wall and his legs swung loosely beneath him. Now the only thing stopping him from falling was his fingers. They were gripping the wooden frame so tightly that Emily could make out the individual bones. And then they started to slip.

Aware that if she didn't do something – and quickly – Robert would be plummeting onto the patio below, Emily lunged forward and grabbed on to his wrists, her fingers feeling sweaty with nerves. If she let go, he'd fall.

She pulled, hard.

'Owww!' Robert shouted.

'Sorry,' Emily panted, her arms aching with the effort. 'You're not exactly a lightweight.'

'It's ... not ... that,' he said.

Emily looked down and gasped. There was blood leaking from two deep grazes where his wrists had scraped against the frame. It was trickling down the windowsill.

'Just open the window,' he pleaded. 'Please?'

If she hadn't been hanging on, Emily would have slapped herself for being so stupid. Why was she trying to pull Robert through the tiny top window when there was a larger one beneath? Idiot. She didn't waste time apologising, but loosened her grip on one of his wrists and, holding on tightly to the other, moved her free hand slowly down to the lower casement. She scrabbled with her fingernails, cursing the fiddly locks, but at last she dislodged the ancient lever and pulled it back.

The window was open.

Grunting and groaning, Robert dragged himself upwards until his legs – as muddy as every other bit of him – were in sight. And then with one supreme effort, he lifted his feet and swung them over the sill. At the last moment Emily remembered to let go of him. He tumbled into the room with an almighty crash and lay in a heap on the floor, breathing heavily.

Emily stared at him speechlessly.

Wow.

Chapter Fifteen

Emily had never had a boy in her bedroom before and certainly not one this dirty . . . or this bloody. 'You'd better come down to the kitchen so I can clean you up,' she said.

He looked at her curiously.

'You might bleed on the carpet,' she said, speaking v-e-r-y slowly in case he was in shock.

Righting himself with difficulty, Robert sat up and stared transfixed at his wrists. 'That would be just great,' he said, his voice slightly uneven.

Before he could pass out – Emily wasn't very good at doing the recovery position, so she couldn't allow that to happen – she grabbed a handful of tissue paper and clamped it round his wrists. 'Come on,' she said.

As she swabbed and cleaned the wounds, which weren't as deep as she'd feared, Emily chatted for Yorkshire. Robert listened as if hypnotised – he was definitely in shock – but she soon discovered that talking to him was like being stuck in a very tricky maze. There were conversational dead ends everywhere.

She couldn't ask him about his parents – he never spoke of them, so it just didn't seem right.

His uncle was a no-go, because she'd heard from Dad when she got back from Haworth that he'd taken a turn for the worse and would be in hospital for at least another fortnight.

And she really wanted to ask about that hug, but felt too embarrassed.

So she kept coming back to the one topic that they seemed to have in common: *Wuthering Heights*.

Hesitantly he began to join in the conversation, telling her that before rehearsals he was so nervous, but that the fear seemed to vanish once he stepped on stage. He was loving the role of Heathcliff.

'How about you?' he asked. 'What's it like playing Nelly Dean?'

Emily screwed up her face. 'It's all right ...' she said uncertainly. 'I know she's a really important character and all that, but—'

'Cathy,' he said. 'That's you.'

Emily paused in her Florence-Nightingale act. He was looking at her in a really weird way. Were those *puppy-dog* eyes ... ? 'No,' she said firmly. 'I'm *Emily*, not Cathy.'

'But you *should* be Cathy,' he said earnestly.

'Really?' said Emily.

'Oh, I ... um ... didn't mean that you were *like* Cathy,' Robert floundered. 'Well, not all the time.' He smiled. 'And I didn't mean what I said about Lexie being a better actress. I was out of order.'

Emily gazed at him dreamily. Oh dear. She was acting more like Isabella, the archetypal wimp, than feisty Cathy whom he apparently adored. As she stared, Robert dragged a hand across his forehead, smearing blood and mud together. Now he looked *really* Heathcliff-esque, sort of wild and uncontrollable ...

Whoa.

Suddenly and in glorious Technicolor™, Emily saw them racing across the moors together, laughing and then shouting and then ... wrapping arms around each other and diving together for a long passionate kiss.

'I'm sorry that I offended you,' interrupted Robert. He was looking deeply concerned. 'I'd love to act with you.'

Ah, *act* with her, not kiss her on a rugged moor. Emily busied herself with the antiseptic wipe so he wouldn't see her disappointment.

'There was something I wanted to ask you,' he added, as she cut the second plaster to size and pressed it firmly into place.

Not sure whether she could trust her voice, she simply nodded.

'I wondered if you'd . . . um . . . help me with my lines after all,' he said. 'I know I sort of lost the plot the other day and I'm sorry.' He paused for a moment. 'Anyway, I thought we could combine it with a . . .'

Latte? Doughnut? Candlelit dinner? Emily leaned forward, wondering if maybe he would kiss her after all.

'. . . bike ride,' he finished.

She sat back again. *A bike ride.* Emily'd been here before. Or rather, she hadn't, because the promised bike ride had never materialised.

'I've got a guest bike,' Robert added. 'How

about it? Are you free next Saturday?' He flashed a disarming grin at her.

No, no, no. She'd look like a tomato after about ten minutes. There was no way she'd ever get to the top of even a single hill.

'Yeah,' Emily said, doing her ditsy grin again. 'Cool.'

With a smile that would melt entire glaciers, he thanked her for the first aid and promised to explain to Dad all about the drainpipe in the morning. And then he was gone.

So high on romance that she was on at least cloud ninety-nine, Emily headed up to bed. Suddenly she had to find out what happened to Cathy and Catherine and Isabella and Linton and . . . Heathcliff. Especially him.

She had a hot date with *Wuthering Heights*.

Two hours later, Emily was finished. And immediately it all made sense. She got it, totally. She *loved* it. She wanted to read it again, like, *now*. And more than anything she wanted it to be next Saturday so she could have a proper, truly romantic rehearsal in the heart of the Yorkshire Moors, where Emily Brontë had written the Best Book Ever.

Chapter Sixteen

It felt like the longest week ever. Freeze-frame by freeze-frame, the days jerked along. There were only two things that made it remotely bearable.

The first thing was Robert. Emily walked to school with him *every single day*. The incident at the window had broken the ice and now they were getting on brilliantly. He was going to kiss her on Saturday, she was sure of it. He was still moody at school but she knew who the real, secret Robert was. He was sensitive and funny and enthusiastic and he lived in her Annexe.

The second thing was the play. Now that she knew Robert really rated her as an actress, Emily was buoyed up by confidence. She'd found the perfect place to practise her lines too: the Arctic dining room. Wrapping herself in a duvet, she shut herself inside its bone-chilling depths and went over and over her lines. It was so worth it. On stage Nelly Dean was mesmerising, her voice resonating with emotion.

Lexie noticed the change in Emily and wasn't happy. 'Hey, play it down a bit,' she hissed after a particularly impassioned exchange between Nelly Dean and Cathy. 'I don't need you stealing the show.'

'Sorry,' muttered Emily.

The strange thing was that Robert seemed to be getting worse and worse. He forgot his lines constantly. In Thursday's rehearsal, when they were doing the last few scenes of the play – the ones where he really got the chance to roar and sulk for Yorkshire – it got so bad that Miss Edwards offered him a script.

'I don't need *that*,' Robert snapped, refusing even to touch the sheaf of paper. 'I'm meant to be *acting*. If I have to read, it's like giving up. I just haven't got my head round the last few scenes yet. All I need is a prompt or two to remind me where we're at.'

The drama teacher raised an eyebrow at him. 'Sure?' she said.

He nodded. 'I'll be better next week, I promise.'

Emily felt a warm glow inside. Whatever was causing the mental block that was stopping him from remembering his lines, they'd sort it out on Saturday. With her help he'd be word perfect again.

Saturday finally arrived.

'Dad says you're going on a bike ride today,' Jenna said at breakfast. 'With Robert.'

'I might be,' Emily muttered. She wasn't fooled for a second by Jenna's innocent tone. And the saintly expression was a dead giveaway. She braced herself.

'I don't get it,' Jenna went on. 'Is he bored of bonding with Dad or something? Why does Robert want to go with *you*?'

Emily shrugged.

'You never go cycling,' Jenna pointed out. She narrowed her eyes. 'Or are you *going out*? Is this Robert's new tactic for infiltrating the Sparrow family? Hey, are you going to *snog* him?'

'*Jenna!*' hissed Emily. She didn't answer the question. She couldn't; she didn't know the answer.

Robert wasn't there, which cut down the

embarrassment factor very slightly. He'd told Emily that he'd meet her in front of the garage, kitted up, and had lent her a pair of deeply unflattering cycling shorts for the occasion, which she was now wearing. They were so big that the waist was as high as a *Pride and Prejudice* dress and the bottom was lined with that stuff Dad used to polish his car. Emily was also wearing a yellow T-shirt, because Maia had told her that this was what cyclists wore, so she bore more than a passing resemblance to a bumblebee. It wasn't her best look.

'So *are* you?' persisted her younger sister. 'Going on a date, I mean.'

'*No*. We are going to practise our lines for the school play,' Emily said slowly and clearly. But inside she was cringing. Not even she thought it sounded remotely credible.

Dad appeared in time to hear this and chuckled to himself. 'Is that what they're calling it this week?' he said, flicking the kettle on. 'Practising lines?'

'Dad!' spluttered Emily, her cheeks hot. Wasn't *anyone* on her side?

He grinned at her. 'Only teasing. You're going out on mountain bikes, aren't you? And you're helping him with his lines. Nice one. That's really kind of you, Emily.'

'Nah,' she said, blushing. It really wasn't that kind, because this was Emily's chance to play the role she'd wanted all along. She'd got into character by leaving her disobedient hair loose – a couple of gusts of wind and it would go wild. Perfect. She knew Cathy's part already – she'd listened to Lexie enough times. And she and Robert would be on a windy moor, which would make it even more amazing.

'Have fun, dear!' said Auntie O, who'd just walked in. 'Don't do anything I wouldn't do.' And she gave a long, slow comedy wink.

'Got to go!' said Emily, before her family could blurt out any more mortifying comments. With as much dignity as she could muster in a pair of Lycra shorts with a padded bottom, she left.

She was going to *be* Catherine Earnshaw.

End of.

They rode away from the house, passing the old church with its moss-covered gravestones. Robert gallantly lifted Emily's mountain bike over the stile that was the gateway to the moors. And he gave her a quick lesson in The Best Way to Ride a Mountain Bike Without Falling Off It. After a few minutes, Emily had got the hang of the gears – why any bike needed twenty-seven of them, she had no idea – and worked out that pedalling hard might be a good way to travel a microscopically short distance at breakneck speed, but if she wanted to get to the top of the moors without turning a pleasing shade of sunburn, then she'd better slow down.

'Steady does it,' said Robert, who wasn't remotely out of breath, despite the fact he was carrying lunch, two scripts and a whole stack of futuristic energy bars in his massive backpack. He radiated encouragement and charm. 'Stay in a low gear and get a rhythm going,' he said softly. 'It's much less tiring that way.'

Grudgingly Emily admitted that he was right. They reached the top of the first slope after about ten minutes and the ground levelled off, allowing her to get some of her breath back. After another ten minutes Emily realised that she was sort of enjoying herself.

'What's the weather forecast?' she asked, admiring the blue sky and fluffy clouds. It was seriously stunning up on the moors.

'Reasonably OK,' Robert said. 'There might be a drop of rain later, but we've got all the gear so that won't be a problem.'

Emily looked down at the waterproof jacket that Robert had loaned her – probably to cut down the glare of her yellow T-shirt – and smiled. She could cope with a little bit of rain.

'Help!' she squealed as her front wheel jolted down a rabbit hole and she wobbled dangerously. But she regained her balance. She was getting good at this. She watched Robert – for technique *and nothing else* – and saw that he stood up on his pedals when he tackled the tricky stuff. So she did the same. With increasing confidence, she negoti-ated hillocks and dips, the grassy ground soft and bouncy beneath her tyres. This was cool.

After another half an hour Robert suggested that they stop for a snack.

'Not yet,' protested Emily, cycling onwards. They'd done endorphins in Science and she knew that they were zinging about inside her right now, because she felt awesome. Emily had always hated sports with loads of rules, but this wild, carefree exercise was something else. She *loved* it.

'Hey!'

Emily looked back to see that Robert had dismounted a way back and was beckoning her. Reluctantly she did a wobbly and very wide U-turn, and headed back towards him. By the time she braked, he was sitting down and rooting through his rucksack. He'd already taken off his black aerodynamic cycling helmet so Emily did the same, plonking her borrowed pink one on the ground beside her. Shaking her hair loose, she was uncomfortably aware that it had gone frizzy inside the sweaty helmet, which wasn't quite the look she'd wanted. She looked up to see that Robert was sucking through a tube that sprouted from his rucksack like a plastic umbilical cord.

'Here,' he said, offering the tube to her. 'It's just water, but in a hi-tech bag. Cool, huh?'

'Er, yeah.' Suspiciously, Emily leaned forward and took the end of the tube. He was still holding on to the rucksack, which meant that she had to move so close to him that she could see exactly how dark his eyes were. Caught in his gaze, she couldn't look away.

She took a slurp of water and promptly choked.

'Are you all right?' asked Robert, slapping her repeatedly on the back.

'I'll ... be ... fine ... once ... you ... stop ... hitting ... me,' gasped Emily.

'Oh,' said Robert. 'Sorry.'

Once she'd got her breath back, Emily decided to broach the subject of the school play. There hadn't been any mention of it since they'd left that morning and it was why they were here after all. 'So, Robert,' she said, suddenly seized by a mischievous urge. 'Or should I call you . . . Heathcliff?'

'Call me what you like,' he said flatly. His good mood had vanished like the sun behind a dark cloud.

'Oh,' said Emily, confused by the sudden change of mood. She tried to repair the damage, though that was tricky given that she wasn't entirely sure what she'd done wrong. 'Sorry. I didn't mean—'

'Oh, it's not you,' said Robert. 'It's me.'

Excellent. Emily had suddenly been transported into the middle of a daytime soap. The last time she'd checked – like, about two minutes ago – they weren't going out. So why was he breaking up with her? 'Pardon?' she said. 'What's not me? What's you?'

'Why I'm moody,' he muttered.

At last. Absolute proof that it wasn't her. A chorus of *Hallelujas* rang inside Emily's head. With difficulty she tried to focus. If it wasn't her, then what was it? 'Yes . . . ?' she said.

'I'm not too good at . . . um . . . erm . . .' He stopped, staring hard at a clump of heather.

Emily leaned forward expectantly.

167

He tried again. 'It's about *Wuthering Heights*...'
And...?

'I... um... well, I can't read the lines without stumbling over them,' he whispered. 'In fact I'm not too good at the whole reading thing full stop.' He shrugged apologetically and then reached into his rucksack and pulled out a crumpled script, which he brandished in one hand. 'My uncle helped me to memorise the audition piece, before he got ill. Then your dad helped me with the first few scenes. He spotted I had a problem when he met me at scouts and he's been brilliant. But he's so busy and I can't keep asking him. And if I can't read my lines, then how can I learn them? How can I be Heathcliff?'

So that was why Dad had been helping Robert and why he'd told Emily that she was being kind. He thought she already knew about the reading. The words came rushing out of Emily's mouth before she could scan them for tact. 'Oh! Is that all?' she said. And then watched awestruck as he began to tremble with rage.

'You have no idea, do you?' he stormed. 'You don't know what it's like.'

Emily shrank back. She'd just been so relieved that it wasn't anything worse, like an incurable disease or something. The last thing she'd meant to do was hurt him.

'It's not a joke,' he said. 'Can you imagine how much of a nightmare it is to go to school and not understand anything that's written down? *You* try looking at a page of meaningless squiggles and watching them dance in front of you and—'

'I'm so sorry,' she interrupted. And she was. *Really* sorry. But it was all beginning to make sense. Of course. Robert *never* read from the script, and he was word perfect, apart from the later scenes that he hadn't yet learned by heart.

'I've been to school after school,' he said, 'trying to hide my problem. Not doing my work, feeling so angry and ashamed that I just want to punch all those people who look down on me, thinking they're better than me.'

Emily felt awful. 'Look, Dad'll be able to help,' she said. 'He knows loads of organisations and groups. He'll know who to talk to—'

'I told you, he knows about my stupid problem already,' Robert cut in. 'And he's been great. He's been helping me learn the rest of my lines,' he went on, 'and he's arranged for extra lessons too, so that I can learn to read properly. He thinks I might be dyslexic or something. People have mentioned that in the past, but I usually moved on before anyone knew for sure. And I haven't got time to wait now. The play is on in a few weeks. I need to be word perfect. I need to know them by heart.' He looked right at her.

'By heart . . .' repeated Emily. His eyes were like pools of dark chocolate. She stared into their depths.

He stared back.

A gust of wind whipped her hair across her face, obscuring her view totally. She pushed the annoying fronds away and gasped – he hadn't been *that* close before. Her insides turned to marsh-mallow. She watched transfixed as he moved closer. And closer.

Chapter Seventeen

Splat.

The wet trickle on her forehead made Emily look upwards. The blue sky was no longer dotted with white fluffy clouds. From horizon to horizon, everything was school-uniform grey. Oh dear. She'd been so sure that he was going to kiss her and now he was sitting far back on his heels. His expression unreadable. Why had he changed his mind?

SPLAT.

A raindrop got Emily right in the eye, jolting her back to reality.

'We're going home.' Robert began packing

away their things. She couldn't see his face, but his shoulders were tense and hunched. He was mad, again.

Emily couldn't work it out. Why did things keep going wrong between them? They hadn't uttered a single word of *Wuthering Heights* yet. She'd been looking forward to today so much, to being Cathy to his Heathcliff. But now she was beginning to think that nothing was ever going to happen with Robert, on stage or off it.

Meanwhile Robert was trying to jam the script back into the backpack and it tore. He swore, loudly, dragging the pile of paper out again. 'I don't need this, do I?' he said bitterly.

Before Emily could stop him, Robert began ripping the pages from corner to corner, tearing out the staples and flinging the pieces into the air. The wind caught them, whipping them far out of reach. He continued until every page was gone.

'Good,' he said.

Emily winced and zipped her jacket right to the top. 'That isn't a drop of rain,' she said, pretending that she hadn't noticed him lose his temper. The elements possessed a powerful beauty and the billowing wind could be seen clearly as it pushed the rain along, sending it whirling and swirling over the moor. She could see the odd sheet of paper, snagged in the heather, now sodden. Here came the rain. Even though she knew she was about to be soaked, Emily couldn't drag her eyes away. 'Look,' she said. 'That's *wuthering* weather.'

'What are you talking about?' snapped Robert.

'Wuthering,' Emily replied. 'You know, like in the book. Being battered by blustery or noisy winds?' A timely gust whipped the green wrapper that she was somehow still holding out of her hand and sent it dancing over the heather.

'*Oh, like in the book!*' mimicked Robert. 'Well I wouldn't know about that, would I?'

Emily scrambled to her feet, wishing that she could wind back time and gag herself. He'd been brave enough to tell her that he couldn't read and she'd repaid him by showing off how much she knew. 'Sorry,' she said.

'Let's just get home,' he said. 'OK?'

The storm struck, making Emily blink with its ferocity. Rain lashed. Wind howled all around. She pulled her hood tighter and tried to ignore the rainwater that was trickling down her bare legs and into her trainers.

'Ready?' said Robert. He slung a long leg over his saddle, clipped his shoe onto the pedal and waited for her, rain dripping off the end of his nose.

Swallowing back tears Emily nodded and, with much less finesse, clambered onto her bike.

'Remember to stick to the tracks, and when you're heading downhill keep your weight well back,' Robert said. He set off.

Emily juddered along after him, trying to keep up. She concentrated hard on the narrow track in front. What was it he'd said? To keep her weight back, that was it. What did that mean? She tried leaning back in the saddle, but it felt dangerous. It couldn't be right. Ahead of her Robert mounted a ridge and then disappeared over the other side. This must be where it got steeper. Experimentally she squeezed her brakes and relaxed a little as she felt them bite. Good. At least she knew that she could stop if she got into difficulties.

As she reached the top of the ridge Emily's courage wavered. Robert was way below. On the way up, the slope hadn't seemed too bad, but from the top it looked like a vertical drop. She breathed deeply to calm her nerves. 'You can do it . . .' she said to herself. 'Girl power and all that, eh?' With trembling fingers, she swept hair away from her face and tucked it inside her helmet. And then she pulled her determined face – clenched jaw, deep frown – that she reserved for moments just like this.

Cautiously she pushed off and tipped over the edge, pointing straight down a narrow track that was shiny with mud. Feeling her speed increase, she pressed gently on the brakes. Her back wheel skidded slightly, but the bike slowed. She went faster, braked and slowed. Over and over. It was a comforting rhythm. Emily was almost starting to enjoy herself when a larger-than-usual hillock appeared in front of her. She headed inexorably towards it. What was on the other side? A slope, a dip or a great big hole? Should she go over it or round it? She didn't know. Gripped by panic, she lurched to the left to avoid the hillock and her front wheel hopped out of the track she was following. She launched into the air.

'*Whoa!*' she shouted. The ground approached with terrifying speed as she tried – and failed – to remember Robert's advice.

Wham! Impossibly, Emily had landed on her wheels. Laughing hysterically, suddenly enjoying herself more than she'd ever thought possible, she rode down the remainder of the slope, hurtling towards a stunned-looking Robert, who was waiting for her. He was smiling and waving at her. She'd actually impressed him.

'*Woo!*' she squealed. 'This is cool!'

Robert was shouting something, but the wind was whistling past Emily's ears too noisily for her to make out the words. He waved again.

Daringly she lifted one hand to wave back, and then hastily replaced it on the handlebars as she realised how rough the ground was at the bottom of the slope. She bumped onwards, fingers resting lightly on the brakes to control her speed. And then she saw it. Beside Robert there was a huge muddy puddle. He pointed at it.

'It's OK,' panted Emily. 'I've seen it!' She imagined the huge plume of muddy water that was going to arch gracefully into the air and land on Robert. Maybe it would cheer him up and give them something to laugh about together.

Her front wheel touched the puddle.

'No!' he cried.

Too late.

It wasn't a puddle. It was a syrupy sticky bog. That was why Robert had been trying to warn her. Emily's front wheel sank on contact and went down, down, down . . . right to the axle, at which point it was clenched in the bog's iron grip. The bike came to a dead halt, but she didn't. She carried on, flying over the handlebars with effortless ease and landing with a loud squelch on her back in the muddy bog.

For a few moments she lay there as the rain pattered gently on her face.

Then Robert appeared overhead. 'Are you OK?' he said, dropping to his knees beside her.

There wasn't a drop of mud on him, which meant that Emily's hilarious plan had been a total failure. But at least he was talking to her now, so maybe the somersault had been sort of worth it. With a great slurping sound, she sat upright. 'I'm fine, I think,' she said.

'The bike isn't,' Robert said simply.

It took precisely two hours and five minutes for them to wheel the broken bike home. After Emily had apologised about a hundred times for wrecking it, there didn't seem much more to say.

But back at the garden gate, Robert interrupted his sullen silence. 'You won't tell anyone, will you?' he muttered. 'About my reading, I mean.'

'Er ... no,' said Emily, 'of course not. But I really would like to help.'

He shook his head quickly. 'That's all right.

Anyway, I shouldn't have told you; it only makes things more complicated.'

'Oh,' Emily replied. 'I see.' She didn't though. And to make matters worse, her conscience was niggling too. Emily had told Dad that she'd help Robert with his lines, and Robert had turned her down. But if she didn't help Robert, did that mean she was letting Dad down too?

It was an impossible situation.

No, actually . . . it wasn't.

A totally genius plan popped into her head: she could make a recording of the entire play using Dad's laptop. It would be Robert's very own audio version. She would burn it onto a CD. And she would give the CD to him. Then he could listen to the dialogue as many times as he liked and learn it, and the best bit was that Emily didn't have to be there, imagining what it would have been like if things had worked out between them.

Fired up, Emily put her plan into action as soon as she'd scraped off the bike-ride mud. She holed herself up in the freezing depths of the dining room, with only Dad's laptop, an old mic, the script and her own misty breath for company.

Three hours later it was done. Taking care to hold the edges lightly, Emily turned the shiny disc to and fro in trembling fingers. She'd read every act, every scene, every line, even the stage directions, so he'd know what he should be doing on stage. It was all on there – every single wuthering word.

Carefully she slid the CD into an envelope and crept up the stairs to the Granny Annexe, praying that Robert wouldn't hear her. She gave the envelope the lightest of kisses. And then she pushed it under his door.

Chapter Eighteen

On Sunday, it rained. A lot. This was excellent as far as Emily was concerned because she needed a watertight excuse if she was going to hang around the house and bump into Robert, and find out if he liked the CD or not. But he didn't appear. There was no sign of him on Monday morning either.

'He went to school early,' Auntie O told a surprised Emily. 'Your dad dropped him off.'

'Typical,' muttered Jenna. 'Didn't offer *us* a lift, did he?'

Emily couldn't care less about the lift, but she was bothered that Robert was clearly avoiding her. Her totally genius plan had failed. Robert hated her. Her sister hated Robert. Maybe everyone else in the house too. Well perhaps she could do something about that. 'I'll walk to school with you,' Emily said.

Jenna looked suspicious. 'Why? So you can cross-examine me on the mysterious disappearance of your Touche Eclat?'

'What?' said Emily.

'Gotcha,' replied Jenna, with a smirk. 'It hasn't disappeared at all. It's right here in my bag. Catch you later, sis!' Waving the telltale gold tube at Emily, she ran for it.

Emily sighed. So much for sisterly kindness.

Robert was at school, as gloomy and gorgeous as usual. Emily was aware of him hovering on the periphery of her vision, but she was too nervous to talk to him. What if he bawled her out? She concentrated instead on making sure that her lines were rock solid, by the simple process of burrowing herself away in the most deserted corner of the library and going over and over them.

It was a full-company rehearsal today – actors, backstage crew, the lot – so by the time Emily got to the school hall it was already rammed. She found Maia on stage.

'Would you just look at that gravestone?' Maia

pointed to the painted cardboard cut-out decorated with an ornate RIP. 'Isn't it stunning? I think it probably encapsulates the whole essence of the play.'

'What, *death*?' Emily frowned at the curved piece of scenery, tried to think of another meaning, and failed. 'Not everyone dies in the book.'

'Don't they?' asked Maia, perplexed. 'I thought they did. Isn't there some sort of plague that nukes all the characters? A sort of literary Black Death?'

Emily laughed. 'No spoilers,' she said. 'Anyway it's all in the script.'

'Ha,' said Maia, 'like I've read that.' She shrugged, unperturbed. 'I can wait until opening night. It will all be a wonderful surprise.'

At the thought of opening night, Emily's stomach lurched. She didn't understand it; how could something so fabulously exciting make her feel so sick? It was bizarre.

'Hello, everyone!' cried Miss Edwards, staggering into the hall carrying bulging black plastic bags.

'Wow, she's brought us Christmas presents,' Maia deadpanned. But she quickly followed Emily down from the stage and joined the crowd swelling around the drama teacher.

'Costumes,' said Miss Edwards proudly. 'Some of them might need a nip or a tuck, but I know you'll all be wowed.' She began handing them out to the actors.

'What . . . is . . . this?' Lexie said slowly, holding a swathe of shapeless dark brown cloth between her thumb and forefinger.

Miss Edwards smiled sweetly. 'It's a dress. Why don't you try it on?'

'I'm Cathy,' spat Lexie. 'Don't I get to wear something a bit, well . . . special, like silk or taffeta or something?'

'Ooh,' whispered Maia, 'a true-life diva.'

'Just try them on . . .' said Miss Edwards tiredly, and Lexie flounced away, muttering.

Emily put on her costume, which was a long grey worsted dress, topped off with a small white cap.

'Yours isn't too bad,' said Maia, screwing up her face.

'Thanks,' said Emily. 'I think.' She performed a twirl and came to a dizzy halt in front of Robert. She smiled at him, unspeakably relieved when he smiled back. She hadn't messed up with the CD and he didn't hate her after all. *Phew*. Everything was going to be just fine. They could be *friends*, at least.

'You look great,' said Robert, his voice deep and gravelly. He bowed stiffly. 'What do you think of my gear?'

Wow.

Her eyes widened. Heathcliff – *no, Robert* – was clad in breeches, riding coat and worn white shirt, looking as if he had just stepped off a moor sometime during the nineteenth century.

'Yeah,' Emily said. She needed to sit down. *Friends? Not in a million years.* She wasn't over him at all. 'Hot,' she said. 'Er, I mean ... that is ... what I meant to say was, um ... *cool*. Wrong temperature. Sorry.'

He smiled warmly.

She melted.

'Um ...' Awkwardly Robert rubbed his fingers down the fabric of his coat. 'I wanted to— *Urgh*!' He sprang away from her.

Emily stared at him in horror. What had she done now?

'Sorry,' he said, pointing to the thin strip of material that ran around the collar. 'Velvet. You know what I'm like with velvet.'

'Act one, scene one!' called Miss Edwards. 'Can I have everyone up on stage who's meant to be there, including stagehands. We're going to do a proper dress rehearsal.'

Anxiously Emily looked from the drama teacher to Robert. 'Yes?' she said breathlessly.

'I just wanted to say . . .' Robert's voice was so low that she could hardly make out the words. 'Thanks.' And then he was strolling towards the stage.

Oh! With a jolt Emily realised that he was talking about the CD. He must have listened to it instead of just chucking it in the bin as she'd feared. 'Hey!' she called after him. 'Good luck with the lines!'

He stopped dead, and then swung round to face her.

Whoa . . . Emily took a step back. Robert's fierce glare made Heathcliff look like a total pussycat. He was furious. 'What did I d-d-do . . . ?' she stammered.

Robert stalked back towards her, his fists clenched tightly.

Emily felt, rather than saw, the rest of the students edge away. All except for Maia who stood at her shoulder, a true friend.

'Why don't you just tell everyone that I can't read?' His voice was as cold and hard as steel. 'Thanks.'

'But, I didn't—' Emily said, her voice rising as she desperately tried to tell him that she hadn't meant that. 'All I said was good luck. I didn't tell anyone that you can't read.'

If anyone had missed Robert's hissed words, they certainly heard Emily repeating them.

'He can't read . . . ?' murmured Maia.

Like ripples from a dropped stone, the whispers spread outwards. Emily watched with dismay as Robert's eyes roamed around the assembled cast and crew, coming to rest on the director. Miss Edwards stared back. So did everyone else.

There was a long, uncomfortable pause during which Robert's hands clenched so tightly that the knuckles went white. Then his shoulders slumped and all the fight seemed to drain out of him. He no longer looked angry. He looked beaten, and very sad. Abruptly he turned to go.

'Robert!' Miss Edwards called after him. 'Wait.'

He ignored her, grabbed his belongings and left, still dressed as Heathcliff.

With the co-star gone there wasn't much point carrying on, and the rest of the rehearsal was cancelled. Miss Edwards said that because everyone had spent so long trying on costumes, they'd run out of time, but they all knew that it was about

Robert. The drama teacher hurried away as soon as the school hall was locked up, a concerned expression ruffling her brow.

And Emily burst into tears.

Chapter Nineteen

Emily was so upset that Maia insisted on walking her home.

'Oh dear,' sighed Emily as they trudged past the mill and the newsagent. 'Oh dear, oh dear—'

'Oh, *shush*!' said Maia, but her voice softened immediately. 'Come on . . . It's not *your* fault.'

'It is.' Emily smeared a cuff across her nose. 'I've told everyone his most secret thing, like, ever and now he hates me.'

Maia shrugged. 'To be fair, he did say it first.'

'I don't think my dad will see it like that,' said Emily. The nearer she got to home, the more worried she felt. Dad had been so pleased that she was helping Robert. Now he would be livid to hear that she'd blown Robert's cover and humiliated him in front of everyone.

Maia waved goodbye at the gate. Grimly Emily walked up the path, and looked through the patterned glass of the back door. The kitchen glowed a warm yellow, she hesitated a moment before going in.

'There you are!' cried Auntie O, looking up from her knitting. 'Robert was home ages ago. We wondered where you'd got to.'

'Um . . . where's Dad?' Emily asked, her stomach churning.

'Upstairs in the Granny Annexe,' said Auntie O. 'Robert wanted to talk to him about something. He didn't look too happy.'

'Oh,' said Emily. *Oh dear. Oh dear, oh dear, oh—*

Just then Dad walked in. His lips were pressed together in a straight line, but the corners curved upwards when he saw Emily. 'Oh, good. You haven't been eaten by wild dogs then.'

'I'm s—'

'Hey, don't worry,' Dad said softly. 'I know the whole story. It was unfortunate how it came out, but it's probably better in the long run.'

'But he must *hate* me . . .' Emily wailed.

Dad shook his head. 'No, love, not at all.'

'What's going on?' asked Auntie O. 'What's Robert doing?'

'He's just packing,' said Dad.

'*Packing?*' cried Emily. Just when she thought things weren't as bad as she feared, they turned out to be apocalyptic.

'Packing?' repeated Auntie O. 'Why? Is the boy going back to his family?'

'Robert's going to stay near his uncle,' said Dad. 'Just for a couple of days, until everything settles down. There's a foster family who'll put him up.'

'What's happened?' said Auntie O. 'I can't help feeling as if I'm a little' – she hooked her fingers in the air – 'out of the loop. Robert's a lovely boy, but he's such a mystery. I'm not even sure why he came to Upton in the first place.'

Emily nodded. She wanted to hear this too. But once Dad had told them, she felt as though she'd just watched a made-for-television film instead.

Robert's parents were actors.

As soon as Emily heard this, clouds parted, sunbeams shone and harp music played. *That* explained where he'd got the fabulous voice from.

They were in theatre – using stage names – and had toured all over the world. Robert had gone with them, attending school after school, never anywhere long enough to learn to read or for anyone to work out that he *couldn't* read. He stayed under the radar, dealing with the constant jibes about his sullen uncommunicativeness. Emily knew exactly what that looked like.

And then Robert's parents decided to produce their own fabulous Broadway play. They ploughed all their money into it . . . and it flopped, big time. They lost everything. Now they were back on the road, trying to pay back crippling debts, but they couldn't afford expensive schools too, so Robert was back in the UK with relatives.

He hadn't seen his parents in months, during which time he'd been thrown out of no less than two schools for his disruptive behaviour. Upton and Uncle Brian were his last hope. If he messed up here, that was it.

The cups of tea had cooled and so had Emily's anger.

'Wow,' she breathed. 'You couldn't make that up.'

'Oh, dear . . .' breathed Auntie O. '*Poor* Robert.'

'This could have been avoided if I'd spent more time with him,' said Dad. He looked sorrowful. 'Story of my life, eh? I'm sure your mum would agree.'

'Don't be silly . . .' Emily gave him a wry smile. She knew that a few extra hours with Mum wouldn't have made any difference, except for giving them more time to squeeze in extra rows. Dad liked helping people. Lots of people. That was just the way he was made.

'Robert tells me that he keeps messing up the last few scenes,' her father went on. 'That's *my* fault. We never got that far.'

But Emily could've helped. If she'd kept her big mouth shut, then Robert could have memorised the rest of the play using her recording. No one would have been any the wiser. He wouldn't be mad at her and then they could have figured out some way for him to learn to read in secret. Oh, and maybe they could have fitted in the soft-focus-falling-in-love bit that was missing from the plot of his life so far. Actually, her life too.

Not any more. She'd ruined everything.

Suddenly Emily knew that she was going to cry. Biting her lip hard, she ran up the stairs to her room. Jenna was there, superglued to Facebook.

Calmly Emily plucked her make-up bag from

its hiding place and handed it over to her sister, who jumped up.

'Can I use *everything*?' Jenna asked, running her fingers over the zip. 'What about the mascara with dual brushes that you banned me from ever touching?' She paused. 'The moisturiser with the alphamax AHAs and provitamin-Z complex that will make me look like a model . . . ?'

'Everything,' said Emily, vaguely wondering how Jenna knew quite so much about her make-up. 'As long as you use it somewhere else. I need to be on my own.'

'Hey, no problem,' said Jenna, tucking the bag into her pocket and grabbing Emily's favourite cardigan. 'Can I wear this too? See ya!'

Footsteps clattered down the stairs. 'Dad, can I go round to Karen's house?' Jenna yelled in the distance.

Emily didn't care that her make-up was going to get more of a hammering than the testers in Boots. She sank down onto the bedroom floor and began to sob. Through her tears she heard the back door slam and the Land Rover rev noisily.

Robert was gone, without a goodbye.

Chapter Twenty

The house was quiet without him.

Too quiet.

Emily hated it. She felt as if the silence was loaded with blame. Dad and Auntie O said that it wasn't Emily's fault, but she knew that probably wasn't what they actually thought. What they were thinking was that she'd stuffed things up royally. Even the velvet sofa looked reproachful. The only person who seemed pleased about it was Jenna.

'We'll get to see a bit more of Dad now,' she said confidently. 'Now that *he's* gone.'

'Right . . .' said Emily.

Auntie O refused point-blank to move back into

the Granny Annexe. 'It just doesn't feel right, dear,' she told Dad. 'We haven't had closure.'

So everyone gingerly avoided the Robert-shaped hole and Jenna stayed in the bottom bunk. Emily stole back the Touche Eclat from under her sister's pillow and used it to cover up the dark circles that came from crying herself to sleep at night.

Of course it wasn't just Robert who'd gone; so had Heathcliff, which was a huge problem as far as the play was concerned.

The day after the ill-fated rehearsal, Miss Edwards gave them the official nod that Robert was dropping out of the play for a few days.

'*What?*' said Lexie, pink with outrage. 'He can't do that. What about *me*? Are you expecting me to rehearse with thin air?'

'Of course not,' said the drama teacher. 'I've already organised for a new Heathcliff for you – someone to fill in for Robert until we sort out what's happening.'

'Who?' demanded Lexie. 'Is it Daniel? It's Daniel, isn't it? Good. Daniel should have been Heathcliff all along. Daniel will be fab—'

'It's Mr Elton,' said Miss Edwards. 'Yoohoo!' she called. 'Come on in.'

What?

Lexie wasn't the only one who was horror-struck.

Emily stared at the drama teacher. Had she gone mad? Mr Elton's voice was fathoms deep and monotonous. He'd given more pupils detention for falling asleep in class than any other teacher. She didn't want *him* to be Heathcliff.

The door creaked open.

'Afternoon,' growled Mr Elton. He didn't look as if he wanted to be Heathcliff either. The physics teacher actually looked as if he'd rather test Newton's theory of gravity by jumping *off* a stage than act on one. His wiry grey beard trembled when he spoke, and his small round glasses magnified the fear in his eyes. The man was clearly terrified.

A splutter-gurgle-choking noise sounded on Emily's left and she realised that it was Maia, trying not to laugh. She failed spectacularly, letting out a gleeful, 'Lexie! You're going to have to snog the physics teacher!'

'Miss?' Lexie pleaded, ignoring Maia. 'I don't, do I?'

Miss Edwards rolled her eyes. 'Of course not.'

Mr Elton looked as if he might pass out with relief.

Emily raised her hand, which refused to stop

shaking. 'Robert will be Heathcliff in the actual play, won't he?' she asked.

Miss Edwards shrugged one shoulder. 'I really don't know,' she said. 'I hope so. But at this late stage if Robert's not around, then *someone* has to play his part. And for now I'm sure Mr Elton will do it wonderfully.' She smiled encouragement at the ghostly pale physics teacher before looking back at the class. One eyebrow arched elegantly. 'Unless one of the other boys would like to volunteer ... ?'

There was a loud shuffling noise as every single boy in the room realised how interesting the parquet flooring was.

'*Daniel!*' said Lexie in a stage whisper. 'This is your chance. You can be Heathcliff, just like you should've been all along. We can act together.'

Daniel shook his head.

'Daniel!' Lexie snapped, crosser now. 'Put your hand up.'

He shook his head again, more firmly this time.

There was a lengthy pause and then Lexie hissed, 'We are so over.'

Daniel didn't look remotely bothered. 'Whatever,' he said.

Lexie's jaw dropped.

'Wow,' said Maia. 'That told her.'

*

Everyone who wasn't oohing and aahing about Lexie and Daniel breaking up or about the new Heathcliff, gossiped about Robert's hasty departure instead.

'Can't he read?' Emily heard one boy saying to another in the cloakroom. 'Wow. Imagine that. No English Lit homework.'

'Dunno,' the other boy replied. 'He can ride a mountain bike though. I've seen him out on his full-suspension kit. It's class. Shame he's not here. I was going to ask him if I could have a go on it.'

They didn't sound bothered at all, Emily realiscd. The reading thing wasn't the big deal that Robert imagined. She just wished he could have overheard them. And she wanted him to come back, more than anything. If she'd blown it with him, fine. She'd have to live with that. But he had to come back for *Wuthering Heights*.

Mr Elton wasn't Heathcliff.

Robert was.

Wuthering Heights seemed to be taking up every waking minute. If Emily wasn't rehearsing with the world's most boring Heathcliff – poor Mr Elton was never going to win an Oscar for his acting – then she was talking about the play or thinking about it. Or thinking about Robert. That was still taking up a huge amount of time. And if she wasn't doing *any* of those things, then she was googling 'stage fright', because even though she was looking forward to the actual performance more than anything, she was stupidly worried that the minute she set foot on stage, she would forget every single word, like at the audition.

Jenna smugly informed Emily that she was acting in her sleep. 'You were saying something about love,' she said. '*That* doesn't sound much like what a servant would be saying. Aren't you supposed to be busy sweeping the hearth or something? I wouldn't have thought you'd be important enough to do the *lurve* thing.' She pulled a face.

Emily ignored her. So what if she was reciting the other actors' lines? That wasn't surprising either. She knew the whole thing by now. Backwards, probably.

Dad wandered into the kitchen holding his mobile. 'Guess what?' he said. 'Go on, guess! I've got some really good news.'

'Inset day!' cried Jenna, leaping up from her chair and waltzing round the kitchen. 'No school and no lessons. *Result!*'

'Unlucky,' said Dad. 'Guess again.'

Jenna slumped back onto her chair and grumbled quietly about nothing being fair around here.

Dad raised his eyebrows at Emily and suddenly she knew. 'Robert's coming back,' she said.

'Is he?' asked Auntie O.

'This afternoon,' Dad confirmed. He was smiling. 'He'll be calling in to get his gear at about five o'clock.'

Oh. Those weren't the right words. Dad must have got it wrong. Why was Robert collecting his stuff? He'd need it if he was moving back in.

Emily's throat was drier than toast. 'He's not staying?'

'That's the best bit,' said Dad. 'Robert's going home. His uncle's well enough to be discharged from hospital today and is expected to make a complete recovery. But he'll need the lad to help out a bit at first. Isn't that great?'

Well, yes and no. It was great that Uncle Brian was on the mend. Obviously. But it was really not great at all that Robert would now be living on the other side of Upton. Now Emily would *never* get the chance to apologise – school was hardly the place for her to pour her heart out – and Charming Robert would be replaced by Miserable

Robert. They'd *never* kiss now. But she couldn't tell Dad that. 'Fabulous,' she said, forcing a smile.

'Yay!' cried Jenna, who'd apparently got over the disappointment of not spending the day watching DVDs and wrecking more of Emily's make-up and had found something else to be thrilled about. 'I can have my room back!' She did a celebratory shimmy.

'Dad,' Emily said, 'how *is* Robert?'

'He sounded pretty good,' said Dad. 'And he told me to say—' His mobile rang again and he shrugged an apology before going through to the hall to answer it. He was still talking animatedly about council cuts when it was time for Emily and Jenna to set off for school.

'Bye!' said Auntie O as they got up to go. She caught hold of Emily's arm and pulled her back for a moment. 'Chin up, dear,' she said. 'Try not to worry about it, whatever it is. These things have a way of sorting themselves out.'

'Yeah ... right,' said Emily. But her mind was whirring so fast that she'd hardly registered Auntie O's kind words. *What had Dad been about to say? What had Robert told him?*

She would ask Robert herself tonight.

*

In Drama that afternoon Miss Edwards announced that although Robert wouldn't be back at school until next week – the final week of term – he'd be coming to Saturday's extra rehearsal. It was to be a proper dress rehearsal with lights and curtains and everything. First night was *that* close.

Emily sighed happily.

Heathcliff was back in the room.

'Bet Mr Elton's doing a happy dance in the science lab right now,' said Maia.

'And what about *Wuthering Heights*?' demanded Lexie, who rather than looking forlorn about her recent break-up, seemed unnaturally hyper. 'If Robert can't read the script, how's he going to act in the play?'

Bzzt. It hadn't been seen for weeks, but Miss Edwards' death-ray stare was as powerful as ever. It sizzled across the classroom.

Emily looked over to check that Lexie wasn't a smoking pile of embers. No, she was simply ashen.

The teacher addressed the room at large. 'I'd be very grateful if everyone could let me worry about Heathcliff's lines and concentrate on their own.'

As they filed out of the classroom after the final

bell, Maia wrapped an arm round Emily's shoulder and gave it a friendly squeeze. 'Hey, how cool is that?' she said.

'*Pretty* cool,' Emily said, somehow managing to sound calm. 'I'm glad he's going to be Heathcliff.'

'Of course you are,' Maia was straight-faced. 'And you don't fancy him at all now, right? I knew that.'

'Good,' said Emily, 'so as long as that's clear.'

'Crystal,' said Maia, with a wink. 'Anyway I'm interested in the play too. Who's going to help him with his lines?'

'Don't look at me,' said Emily. She checked her watch: four o'clock. He'd be at home in an hour. 'Sorry, there's somewhere I've got to be,' she said. And legged it.

A few minutes later Emily was pounding up the hill, nervous excitement fizzing inside her. She hadn't seen Robert since that awful day in the school hall. It seemed like years ago now. How would he act towards her? Had he really forgiven her? Dad had told her that Robert didn't blame her, but what if he did? Totally out of breath, she crashed through the gate and stumbled to a halt by the back door. With trembling fingers she fed her key into the lock, pushing the door open to see . . . Dad.

She checked out the kitchen. Definitely no Robert.

'Sorry, love. You just missed him,' said her dad. 'He came early, packed the stuff into his uncle's car and rode his bike home. Says he'll be back to pick up the spare bike when he gets a chance, but he didn't say when that would be. Still, you'll see him at rehearsals, right?'

'Yeah,' said Emily.

Curses.

Chapter Twenty-one

Emily wasn't quite sure how she made it to Saturday without exploding, but she got there unscathed, at least outwardly. But inside she was a mess, frazzled with trying to figure out what Robert might have said.

When she'd asked Dad, he'd said, 'Something about music, I think.'

But that made no sense at all.

Music? They'd talked – OK, argued – about a lot of things, but music wasn't one of them. None the wiser and filled with trepidation, she walked into the school hall on Saturday. The first thing she saw was the cast and crew of *Wuthering Heights* gathered around Robert.

She stopped dead.

He looked totally hot. No change there, then. But something was different. Was he taller? No . . . He'd only been away a couple of weeks. Then she saw, Robert wasn't moping in a corner. He wasn't scowling. He was chatting to the others, even smiling a little, and reminding her very much of someone else she knew from home: Charming Robert.

Emily's mood lifted. And then fell again. Who was she kidding? Robert might be being charming to everyone else, but he hadn't seen her yet. She wanted to go over and apologise for letting his secret out, but she held back. What if she extended her olive branch only for him to fling it back at her?

No way.

Emily hung back and pretended to read her script, by now every line so ingrained in her memory that she didn't think she'd ever forget a single wuthering word.

As soon as Miss Edwards arrived and called them all to order, Robert broke away from the others. He caught Emily's eye and gave her a long, searching look that made her stomach somersault. He didn't *look* angry. She tried to smile at him, but it felt like that time the dentist had numbed her mouth and all she could manage was a gawp.

'Attractive,' observed Maia.

Emily pointed her nose in the air and marched past Robert towards the girls' changing room. She found her outfit quickly and pulled on the worsted dress. *Excellent.* She felt better wearing her Nelly Dean disguise, braver somehow.

The rehearsal began.

Maybe it was the contrast with Mr Elton, but Emily blinked at the brilliance of Robert's performance. He was angrier, louder, wilder. There was no stuttering; he knew it all. And because he was more confident, Emily began to relax and concentrated on making sure that her own performance was as good as it could be.

The only person who wasn't brilliant was Lexie. Her mood seemed to have plummeted and she stumbled through her lines, blaming everyone else for putting her off. Close-up, Emily saw that her eyes were red-rimmed and sore-looking and she couldn't help feeling almost sorry for the girl. Splitting up with Daniel must be hitting her hard.

Once or twice Robert prompted his co-star,

which made Emily's eyes snap open. Was it because of her recording that he knew the play so well? Or had someone else helped him? She wished she'd been brave enough to ask.

'I can read the lines myself, thanks,' Lexie snapped at Robert, snatching a script from one of the lighting technicians, 'unlike some people around here.' She stomped to the back of the stage and mouthed words silently for a few seconds.

Everyone waited.

Emily glanced at Robert quickly. He was concentrating on his feet, which meant that she had no way of gauging his reaction to Lexie's cruel snipe.

Lexie whirled round and stormed back onto the stage, crying, 'Heathcliff!'

Or that's what Lexie *would* have done, if her foot hadn't caught in a neat coil of wires backstage. She tripped and fell. Her hands flailing, momentum carried her forward, her loud, '*Heathclarrrrggghhh—*' curtailed as she hit the stage with a sickening *thump*.

Emily winced.

'Are you OK, Lexie?' called Miss Edwards from the school hall, where she was watching the rehearsal.

Robert rushed over and crouched down beside his co-star.

'Owww . . .' moaned Lexie. 'It's my ankle. I've broken it, I know I have. It hurts *so* much . . .' She began to cry.

Maia looked bored. 'Drama queen,' she mouthed at Emily.

'Don't worry. I'm sure it's not that bad.' The drama teacher jogged up the steps to the stage. 'Let me see.'

'Erm . . . Miss Edwards?' said Robert, who had gone a weird shade of yellowy-green. 'Actually her ankle doesn't look too clever. It's sort of wonky.'

Miss Edwards kneeled down beside Lexie and was silent for a moment. And then she spoke in a terrifyingly calm voice. 'Right, dear,' she said, 'I think we'll get someone to take a look at that.'

By Monday morning, Lexie was encased in pink plaster from her knee to her toes because her ankle was well and truly broken. And she was out of the play.

'It's terrible news about Lexie,' said Miss Edwards to the class. 'I'm sure we all wish her well.'

Everyone nodded, Maia more vigorously than most.

Terrible.

'But it also means that we're one Cathy short of a *Wuthering Heights* cast,' Miss Edwards went on, 'and the play's only four days away. I need a new Cathy, and quickly.'

There was silence as everyone took this in.

Emily gulped. She wanted to volunteer, she really did. But she couldn't do it, not after everything that had happened between her and Robert. He wouldn't want her to star in the play with him. She'd blown his cover. He—

'Miss?' interrupted a dark-chocolate voice from the back of the classroom. 'Emily can do it. She's a brilliant actress. She helped me to learn my lines and I'm pretty sure she knows the rest of the play back-to-front too. *She's* your Cathy.'

Miss Edwards smiled serenely. 'Wonderful idea, Robert,' she said. 'And, I must admit, *exactly* what I was thinking myself. Emily, what do you think?'

Emily nearly fell off her seat. They both thought she should be Cathy?

This wasn't wonderful. This was *perfect*!

Before the next rehearsal, Emily plucked up the courage to thank Robert for bigging her up to Miss

Edwards, to which he gruffly replied, 'It made sense. You're the best one for the job.'

'Well, thanks anyway,' said Emily. She'd sort of hoped that it might have been because he liked her, but if he thought she was a good actress, then that was cool too.

'Anyway, you helped me,' Robert added, unexpectedly.

'Huh?'

'The CD,' he prompted.

'Oh,' said Emily. 'That's, er . . . great.'

'Didn't your dad tell you?' Robert frowned. 'When I picked up my stuff, I asked him to tell you how much I liked the CD. I listened to it so many times, I was worried I might wear it out.'

The truth dawned.

Dad had got it wrong. Robert's message hadn't been about music at all. Her father must have assumed that Robert was talking about a music CD, not the audio CD she'd recorded.

Robert liked it.

She felt like running over and hugging him.

But she couldn't because Robert was too unpredictable. What if Miserable Robert resurfaced? Miss Edwards chose that moment to call all the actors on stage for another announcement.

The drama teacher waited until they were all gathered round. 'I'm sure you all realise that we're still an actor short,' she said.

'Are we?' whispered Emily to Robert. Somehow, he was still beside her and she couldn't think about anything else. 'Who's that?' she asked Miss Edwards.

'Er . . . Nelly Dean?'

Ah.

Everyone stared at Emily.

'What?' she spluttered. 'Give me a break. I can't play both parts.'

'Which is why *I* am going to do the honours,' said the teacher, smiling proudly at them all. 'On Friday, Year Ten, *I* will be Nelly Dean.'

After a brief, stunned silence, they began to clap.

It was going to be a memorable performance.

The last few rehearsals were a mixture of nerves and brilliance. Emily's nerves. Robert's brilliance.

If it hadn't been for the pleasant soft-focus haze that took over every time she was with Robert, Emily would have been sick of the sight of him. On top of rehearsals they spent break times, lunchtimes, every spare moment practising their lines. And because of *Wuthering Heights*, there was no time to discuss anything apart from the play. But the hours they were putting in were making a difference, everyone said so. 'You've got a certain chemistry,' Miss Edwards told them on the night of their last rehearsal, making Emily blush. The question was: *would that be enough?*

The day of the performance arrived.

Emily was bricking it. She stood backstage wearing the costume that the former Cathy had ridiculed for being tight and ugly, but actually fit the new Cathy quite well. This was it. She heard the rumble of the audience as they sat, chatting and fidgeting beyond the velvet curtain. She pulled back the fabric and looked out at the sea of faces. There was Dad on the end of a row, and beside him was Auntie O, and there was Jenna and . . . Mum! Emily nearly squealed with excitement. They were all sitting on the same row. For one night only, her family was together and Emily was on stage. Playing the lead.

Jenna had spotted her and waved furiously.

Emily grinned back at her sister, who had returned to her normal annoying self now Robert wasn't living with them any more. She let the curtain drop. It wasn't long now.

'Hey,' said a low voice.

Emily turned and saw Robert. In the dim light backstage, wearing his super-swarthy make-up and Heathcliff gear, he looked more fanciable than ever.

'Hey,' she laughed. 'Keep away from the curtains. They're velvet, you know.'

He smiled but didn't say anything.

'Are you all right?' she whispered.

'I . . . yes, I'm fine,' he said. 'It's just that, well, the thing is that, um . . . there's something I wanted to say to you.' He stared right at her. 'I've been trying to say it ever since I got back.'

Emily gulped. 'You have?'

'Do you know why I listened to your CD so much?' he said softly.

'Because you wanted to learn the words?' she replied.

'Well, yeah,' he admitted. 'That was the reason at first. But I know all of the words now, and I still listen to it.'

'Oh,' said Emily, wishing that this conversation were scripted as well as the play, because Robert was coming out with all the best lines here. Although the truth was that she didn't know *what* to say. She hadn't a clue where this was going and didn't really care. She only knew that she was enjoying being this close to Robert very much and that she didn't want it to end.

'I love your voice,' he grinned. 'Even if you do talk rubbish most of the time. I've always loved it, actually. Ever since you mouthed off at Miss Edwards in class on my very first day.'

Emily stared at him, wondering for a moment if she was so stage-frightened about the play that she'd passed out and was dreaming all of this and was going to wake up in A&E or something. 'But why didn't you say anything before?' she asked. 'What about all the times we've been up on the moor? You could have told me then, instead of losing your rag at me.'

'Yeah, I know,' he said, looking contrite. 'I'm sorry. But I was just too messed up and angry about my reading and Uncle Brian and everything. I lashed out.'

'OK, but—'

He grabbed one of her hands. 'Now I know you've got a great voice and everything, but will you please shut up so I can kiss you?'

Emily grinned. 'Oh, all right then,' she said.

Robert's lips touched hers, gently at first and then ... *Oooh*. It was *amazing*. He wrapped his arms tightly around her and it didn't seem to matter that they were in a dark corner backstage, which wasn't anywhere near as romantic as a wet, wild, windy moor. But stuff that. She would kiss this boy anywhere.

Emily pulled away and smiled up at her co-star. 'I hate to break this up,' she said. 'But I think there's somewhere we need to be right now.'

Robert glared furiously at her.

'What's wrong *now*?' Emily asked.

'Just getting into character,' Robert said, dodging her punch.

The lights went down and the curtains drew back.

Cathy winked at Heathcliff.

Show time.

Jane Airhead

Kay Woodward

A *Bridget Jones's Diary* for teens. Thirteen-year-old Charlotte is obsessed with Jane Eyre. She dreams of living in a gothic mansion in the Yorkshire countryside instead of attending Harraby Comprehensive School, where nothing exciting ever happens. She decides to find a Mr Rochester for her mum, and her prayers are answered in the form of a dark, handsome new French teacher!

But Charlotte has to control her hopes of being a bridesmaid, because Mr Grant turns out to be not nearly as charming as his sideburns had promised. Has she set her mum up with an evil, philandering bigamist?

A brilliantly witty account of the trials of an imaginative thirteen-year-old girl, with a classic twist!

'A humorous look at teen life and relationships' *Bronteblog*

9781842709764 £5.99